ROD STRING NAIL CLOTH

AN AFROFUTURIST MIXTAPE

T. AARON CISCO

Copyright © 2021, Taylor A. Cisco, III

All rights reserved.

ISBN: 9798702130040

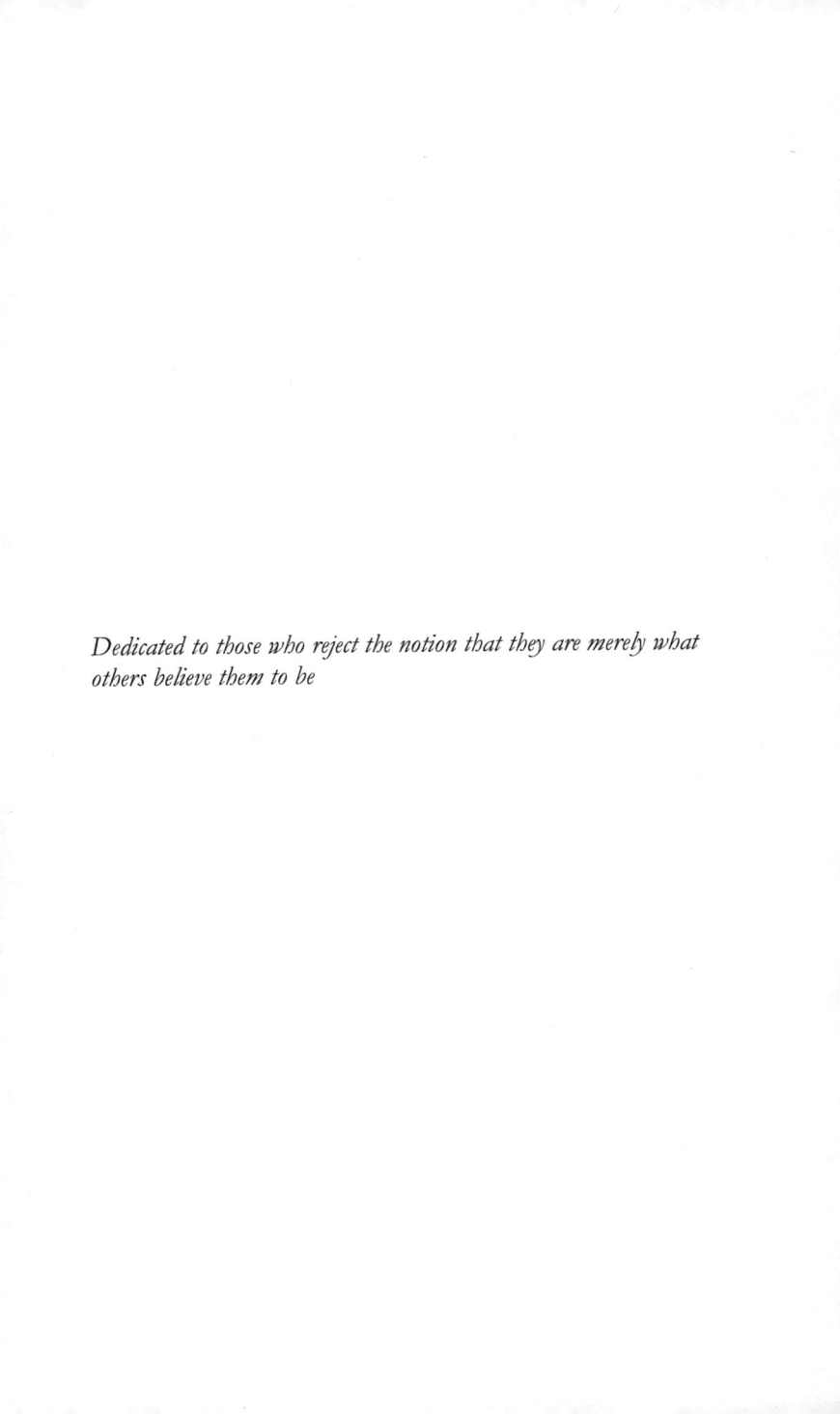

Dedicated to those who reject the notion that they are merely what others believe them to be

TABLE OF CONTENTS

NOW, JUSTICE *(p7)*

THURSDAY ADDISON *(p31)*

THE HESITANT ENVOY (*p59*)

THE LYDIAN MODE (*p79*)

CAPTAIN MICHAELA (*pg117*)

ROD STRING NAIL CLOTH (*pg125*)

THEY BURN SO EASILY (*p153*)

ROD STRING NAIL CLOTH

Now, Justice

T. AARON CISCO

When I was eight years old, I was still having trouble trying my shoes. I couldn't consistently get the knots to stay put, and on the occasions that I did get them secured, they weren't very tight. I was at a pool looking at the inflatable donuts they gave to us kids who weren't strong swimmers and thought how great it would be if they made a tiny version of those innertubes and put them in sneakers. That would remove knots from the equation and be the answer to my shoe tying woes.

The next day at school, I told my classmates and teachers. The nice kids said people wouldn't want tiny inflatables in their shoes, when it only took a few seconds to tie knot. The mean kids just said I was dumb.

A few weeks later, the exact same people who'd told me how dumb I was, showed up to school wearing Reebok Pumps- a sneaker with a little button in the tongue that you'd press to inflate little chambers throughout the shoe to increase and decrease the tightness for the preferred fit.

When I was twelve years old, I was running errands with my parents and got annoyed by how long it took to pay for our groceries. It wasn't that there were too many people in the queue, it was just a handful of customers holding us all up. Someone wanted to chat with the cashier. Someone wanted to use a personal check. Someone didn't read the coupon's expiration date and wanted to argue.

At this particular grocery store, I noticed that the cashier only handled the monetary transactions. At the end of the counter, customers had to bag their own groceries- which also contributed to the long wait times. I thought to myself, if every other aspect of this trip was self-service, why not the cashier? We'd retrieved and returned the shopping cart. We'd selected our items from the aisles and displays. We'd bagged our groceries. It didn't make any sense that this one aspect required an in-person interaction.

I told everyone I could about my idea of an automated cashier station, and just like before with the sneakers, they all laughed. Even my closest friends, who'd eventually admitted my sneaker idea was good, said this was too far.

By the time I had finished high school not only were self-service check outs not *too far*, they were commonplace. The stores still had live cashiers, but by the time I got to college, the automated stations were equal to, or in some cases, outnumbered their flesh and blood counterparts.

Speaking of college, my second year saw not one, but two ideas disparaged by both friends and acquaintances, only to be adopted by the masses a short time later. I'd found a passion for the visual arts and had even shot a handful of short films. I'd considered pursuing a career in independent filmmaking, when I realized how serialized television could be the next big movement in entertainment.

I'd discovered and watched most of my favorite shows on DVD. I didn't have cable, so I'd wait until summer, after the regularly scheduled broadcasts had ended, and would voraciously consume a season or two at a time. I thought about how great it would be if new show content was produced like this as well. Instead of shooting and releasing an episode per week, just produce an entire season, all 13 to 26 episodes, then release them all at once.

I also thought that instead of going to a video store,

there could be ATMs for DVD rentals. My friends laughed at me again. And then, just a few months later, DVD rental kiosks popped up everywhere. Soon after that, the expression, "binge watching," entered the common lexicon.

It was at that exact moment I understood that the truth of the matter. It wasn't that people didn't like my ideas. People just didn't like me. However, it was also in that moment that I realized, I didn't care whether or not people liked me. I just needed a way to bring my ideas to fruition.

I'd become a seasoned observer of the mainstream. My vantage point was a perpetually reserved, immovably affixed seat far on the outside. From this perch looking in, I began to notice a few recurring patterns. I didn't fully understand it, but I saw a common theme running throughout my fleeting glimpses of middlebrow existence.

I trained myself to be unwaveringly focused. If I wasn't learning something new, I was reinforcing my existing knowledge and honing my skills. Reaching my objective wouldn't be possible or practical via sprint, or even a marathon. This was a lifelong excursion.

I'd spend entire afternoons just observing. I'd eavesdrop on conversations ranking from gut-wrenchingly mundane, to soul-crushingly notorious. I watched those who'd already gotten to where I was trying to be and memorized their habits and speech patterns. I'd copy their mannerisms and sartorial choices. I noticed right away the difference between those who had, those who wanted, and those who were just posing. Within a few years, it was no longer an act. It was seamless mimicry.

The posers were comical, perplexing, irrational, hateful, mundane, and predictable. They reveled in their own hypocrisy, and championed fraud, but simultaneously, claimed to respect and desire authenticity. It was not about actually being, but rather pretending to be.

Optics are important, sure. And it's hard to argue against the notion that our individual perception shapes the collective reality. And when those perceptions ran contrary to provided, irrefutable evidence, instead of accepting and learning, I found that the vast majority of people ignored the truth without any hesitation.

They'd all agree that less time needed to be spent focusing on appearance, and more on improvement, but very few actually changed behaviors, or even redirected their focus towards actionable goals and objectives.

Their lives were wasted in pursuit of status symbols, rather than actual status. But status symbols are just that- symbols. And symbols only have the value and meaning we attribute to them; thus, they are, in essence, meaningless. True status is shown by intangibles like power, influence, political capital, authority, respect.

Like Warhol once said, the greatest thing about America is that merchandise is the great equalizer. A Coke is a Coke. Anyone from the Queen of England to bottom of the barrel can buy a Coke. In both cases, a Coke is a Coke.

And that's the way it is across the board for every status symbol. It might take a bit longer to pull the funds together, but anyone can buy anything. And since anyone can buy anything, it's the stuff that money can't buy that really determines clout.

It's why my work is so important. You can't make right, without first identifying what's wrong. Even though the overwhelming majority of my fellow Americans choose to reject, ignore, or even just take a few moments to educate themselves about what's wrong, I must prevail.

History is supposed to be cyclical, in the sense that it's infinite. But what we've established over the past century and a half or so, is less a timeline painted on a mobius strip, and more a tally etched into the back of an ouroboros.

I mean, it's been nearly two hundred years since Emancipation, and look at how they treat us. It's become routine. They harass, beat, intimidate, brutalize, and kill. One gets called out for their tyranny. A few folks make speeches. And then they harass, beat, intimidate, brutalize, and kill us again.

Has there been progress? Sure. But if this was a junked car, we've merely painted on a fresh coat paint and patched up a hole or two. But it's the car is still broken. No amount of surface cleaning and polish is going to get the engine running so we can get to where we need to go.

We can't keep allowing the leadership to do the same thing, all the while hoping that this time will be different. If we want real change, then the responsibility is on our shoulders alone. We're the only ones with the capability. And we must do it. Because what has been, absolutely can no longer be. Not anymore.

The trajectory of our country is well-past the center point. We're not a doomed ocean liner about to hit an iceberg, nor are we shooting off flares after the collision, scrambling to save the passengers and crew. The residents of our borders are floating on the same, chunk of wood. Some of us have drowned. Some are desperately fighting fatigue. Many others have succumbed to extreme hypothermia. The ocean liner is rapidly descending beneath the unforgiving waves and will never float again.

But realizing this fact isn't tragic. On the contrary, it's an opportunity. It was a bad boat to begin with. It didn't provide equitable accommodations or considerations for the passengers. It was bloated and unwieldy, lacking the most basic common-sense contingencies

We shouldn't want, nor should we try to salvage or rebuild the broken, sunken wreck. Survivors shouldn't use the archaic specifications to recreate the same mechanisms and conditions. We have the means to construct a better, smarter, safer vessel. What's lacking is the motivation.

We must abandon the mindset of the archaic. We must understand that all notions of identity are symbolism. There's no gay or straight or masculine or feminine. They are superlatives. Like all superlatives, at best they are useless.

Attributing value to that which is valueless is an exercise in puerile distraction. It's time to stop kneeling at the altar of false equivalence. The lionization of the superfluous must be completely discarded.

Crimefighting is easy. The only two ingredients needed to commit a crime are motive and opportunity. If either is missing, then there's no crime. If someone is unable to break the law, or doesn't want to, then in nearly every case, no law gets broken. Even in a group setting, an unmotivated criminal is at best, a reluctant accomplice. If one member of the team lacks the will or tools to do it, then again, in nearly every case a crime will not occur.

Because of this, a crimefighter need only to remove one of the ingredients. Motive is the more challenging of the two- considering the inherent self-destructive nature of mankind, but by focusing on the opportunity, criminality can be curbed to a near non-existent level.

Fighting oppression however, is nowhere near as straightforward as crimefighting. Oppression is a systemic trait, requiring vast numbers of passive and active members to be aggressively complicit.

Therein lies the rub. I'm just one person. And that old adage about how all it takes to make a difference is one person? There's no historical precedent or evidence supporting that inspirational garbage.

Another year, another idea. They don't laugh at me, because I don't share the concept. Instead I dive into research and experimentation. Weeks turn into months, and months stretch on further than expected. Finally, a breakthrough. Build the prototype housing with the 3D printer. Assemble the components. Embed the device and run the tests. Success.

It disrupts and interferes with the Parietal, Occipital, Temporal, and Frontal regions. By manipulating the senses. I can become someone or something else. I can anyone experience whatever I want them to. What we perceive is our reality, and I've mastered the mechanisms of perception. I call it, The Veil. Time for a field run.

The lines had been drawn centuries ago. Generation after generation they began as predators and oppressors, and over time perfected their malevolent craft, constantly pushing against the edge of what was tolerable.

This one though? He didn't just breach the perimeter of begrudgingly acceptable. He leapt arrogantly over the border with a dehumanizingly reckless abandon.

I am no longer Kodyn Lennox, the thirty-eight-year-old, Black man with broad shoulders and a square jaw. Tonight, I'm a twenty-two-year-old, white woman with strawberry blonde hair, slender hips, and hazel eyes that I call 'Celeste.'

Celeste is effective bait. The smug personification of inhuman hubris with coarse blonde hair started following me eight seconds ago. He doesn't know that I'm not lost. He thinks that I'm intriguing. I'm both the opposite and opportunity he's been looking for.

He sees a damsel awaiting rescue by a white knight in body armor. A distraction that he could safely retreat to the shadowy comforts, hiding beneath the privilege of power. But what he sees is as false as the motto painted in reflective letters across side of his transport.

His pallid eyelids don't blink so much as periodically slide together and slither apart. His clay is still soft. He hasn't been hardened in the kiln. Though deliberately molded and shaped, he's never faced any real heat.

The brittle wind breaks through the mirage, and lap their cold, dry tongues against my true skin. The weather is seasonal and drives most to seek the safety of shelter. To me, this is perfect. The lower temperatures and frigid breeze are a siren's call, reverberating through frostbitten ears. The winter is a leash of braided iron, coiled tightly around my soul. The ruthless pulling is as satisfying as it is necessary.

Celeste offers exceptional camouflage. As I suspected, he didn't notice anything out of place about a petit, white woman. The powers make their assumptions based on assigned notions of value. The merit of value is determined based on the shell. To them, an uncracked egg in the hand is easier to digest than bowls of albumen and yolk. Though the former offers less options for sustenance.

I let him pull up next to me. He flashes his lights, so I stop and turn. He tosses up a friendly wave as he casually slides his husky frame out of the cruiser, sucking in his belly as he struts around the car over to me. Reflexively, I look at his hands. They're empty.

In my true form, the fingers on one of his hands would have been wrapped tightly around the rubberized grip of his sidearm, while the fingers of the other would be clenched and trembling, locked in a fist of hateful rage, or extended like talons in an accusatory point.

He holds a soft expression only because he can't see my real face. If he could, his mouth wouldn't curve up at the corners. His eyes wouldn't be kind. No, his mouth would be wide and feral, baring serrated teeth and vomiting otherworldly profanities. His pupil-less eyes would've been ringed with fire and rage, the same as they were last Fall, when he murdered Demarcus Wilkins, a young man whose only crime was wrong place, wrong time, wrong color.

To keep up appearances, the officer's superiors put him on leave pending an investigation. What precisely it was that they were investigating is the real mystery, since the entire incident, like hundreds of others before, and hundreds if not thousands that will tragically follow, was recorded and livestreamed to millions of eyewitnesses in real time.

The authorities decided that no crime was committed. No repercussions would follow. The family of the deceased, and all of us who lived in the perpetual shadow of oppression and degradation, had no other options but to accept their ruling as final. It was all the more tragic because it was so predictably cliché.

A person of color has a fatal interaction with a law enforcement officer. The story breaks. Demonstrations ensue. Politicians make speeches, calling for investigations. Eventually, the case is settled, and the surviving family is awarded a monetary payout.

Then a few weeks or months pass. Another person of color has an interaction with a law enforcement officer, during the course of which, the law enforcement kills the person of color. The story breaks, and there's some public outrage, and so on and so on, ad infinitum.

Bigots try to paint the oft-repeating tragedies as isolated incidences, as though the same atrocities happening to the same group, by the same oppressors is mere coincidence.

That badge hanging from his belt makes him no more a noble officer of the peace than the leather on my boots make me a snake. Policing is his job. It's a title he holds, a weapon to brandish. I don't want this because he is. I want this because of what he did. And to be clear, I don't want revenge. I want justice.

"Hey there!" he called out, his voice filled with the patronizing arrogance that can only be acquired after years acquittal from unanswered atrocities and wanton bigotry.

"Hello." I responded quietly, allowing my lips to curl ever so slightly at the edges.

"It's a bit cold out to be walking, huh?"

"It's not that bad." I coyly lean forward.

"What happened, car trouble? I could give you a lift."

"Oh, that's all right. I don't' want to impose." I tilted my chin down, pull a few locks of blonde hair behind my ear, and look up at him with unblinking eyes.

"No trouble at all." he smiled, "Not to mention, a distress alert just went out. Can't have a pretty thing like you our here all alone."

He jogged around to the passenger side and opened the

door. As I slip inside the police cruiser, I bristled slightly from the jolt of overheated air blasting from the vents. In the heat, the smell of spicy stale cologne and an over the counter, upholstery cleaning fluid.

The pungent blend and causes me to recoil, and my awkward recoil briefly interrupted the signals from the Veil. I felt the disguise slipping, and quickly looked into the rearview mirror. For the briefest moment, the dark eyed, mocha-tinted visage of my true appearance stared back at me. I shook it off and forced myself to focus. Adjusting the settings on the Veil, Celeste quickly reappears in the mirror, just as he slips into the driver's seat.

"So," he grinned slimily, "Where you off to?"

"Oh uh," I bit my lower lip seductively, "I was actually just looking for a place to get a drink. I'm not from around here. I'm staying back at the Ruby Cottage Inn."

"Wow, Ruby Cottage?" he smirked as he pulled away from the curb, "How'd you get all the way over here? I mean, that's one hell of a walk."

"You're telling me!" I chuckled, the Veil masking my baritone guffaws, so they sound like soprano giggles, "The bar next door, wasn't really my style."

"You must be frozen solid, huh?" Reaching over, he placed his hand on my left knee and squeezed gently, letting his palm linger, "Look at how cold you are."

"I could really use something to warm me up." I winked.

I gently grabbed his wrist. Crossing my legs towards him, I placed his hand on my outer thigh. He arched his eyebrows with a lascivious grin and pretended to get an idea.

"Oh, I know a place where you can get a drink."

"Oh yeah?" I slide his hand higher up my thigh.

"Just wait."

Soon, we've left the semi-spacious landscape of the commercial office parks dotting the suburban landscape and are cruising the streets of downtown Minneapolis.

Minneapolis is a city that thrives on denial. Denial of opportunity. Denial of equity. Denial of history. It's the latter point that's most apparent as he pulls into the alley behind the artist lofts. It wasn't that long ago that these lofts were factories, shops, and other economic cornerstones.

Now, they were monuments to faux altruism. Towering landmarks offering luxurious accommodations in otherwise unobtainable neighborhoods to those trying to make a living in the creative arts. Of course, the truth wasn't exactly as aligned with the clever ad copy of the brochures. Even a passing glance at some of the tenants and their cars, revealed that many of the "starving" artists were anything but.

To maintain some semblance of reverence, the loft buildings retained some of the previous attributes of their former purpose. Like a lot of newer construction projects at the time, the exterior architects and interior designers used weathered brick, concrete flooring, negative space, and exposed ductwork to hinted back to the industrial roots of their contemporary golems.

Photos the buildings in their past glory dotted the walls. Industrial themed sculptures of indeterminate purpose and intention littered the common areas. Even the parking lot blended modern conveniences with a pre-WWII aesthetic. The sensors to activate the parking gates were hidden within bronze placards and iron stanchions.

"Hey, aren't you that cop from the news?" I ask, "The one that shot that boy."

"Yeah, that boy…" he sucks breath though clenched teeth, but doesn't take his hand off my leg, "The media and wannabe activists tried to make it like I'm some kind of racist, like I was looking for an excuse to shoot. But they weren't there. They don't know what really happened."

"So, what really happened?" I purred.

"Just because he was unarmed, doesn't mean he's not dangerous" he smirked, "I mean, it's not like they're going to tell you if they're criminals or not. And besides, if he wasn't doing anything wrong, he shouldn't have run. You don't seem like one of those 'Justice for Demarcus' folks. Someone like you, probably waited for all the facts, right?"

"Oh, for sure." I assured him, keeping my rage in check.

"So, you know this wasn't some Eagle Scout or choir boy. Kid had smoked weed, done some shoplifting. That boy was going to grow up and be a menace. I'm not saying I'm glad I shot him. But if I had to do it again? I would."

We pulled into a loading dock between two of these loft buildings, driving just deep enough in so as not to draw attention from the nonexistent passerby. At this hour, the streets were empty save for a few homeless folks in various states of mental distress and chemical dependency, who sought shelter from the wind as they paced the spaces between towering edifices of glass, stone, and steel.

His relentless pawing was voracious and confident. It was obvious that I wasn't the first to whom he'd offered a "friendly" ride on a cold night. Whatever misgivings I might have had at the beginning of the night vanished the moment he began pawing at my shirt.

I deactivated The Veil. He continued pawing at me but slowed when he realized his face was no longer buried in the sumptuous flesh of pale, pinkish cleavage, but rather mashing against the hardened and swarthy contours of my own barrel chest.

"What?!" he recoiled in horror, "How the hell did you!"

"Evening officer." I smirked, "Justice for Demarcus."

I used The Veil to make him believe that his hands were

cuffed, the car was on fire, and he was burning alive.

His psyche fractured under the pressure. He brain was on terrified autopilot. His neural processes were trying desperately to rationalize the new reality in front of him, rebooting through reflexive vocalizations.

A common misconception is that psychosomatic conditions lie solely in the mind. The brutally grim fact of the matter is that the physical effects are very real. Because his mind believed he was burning, he was. I was simply reversing the process of perception. Instead of the sensory receptors sending signals to his spinal cord and brainstem, then on to his brain to register the agonizing sensations, the perception of charring flesh originated in his parietal lobe and was electrifying his nerve endings. His heartrate increased as he hyperventilated. Within seconds he'd go into shock, and his functions would be compromised.

The pain he believed he was experiencing paled in comparison to the pain he'd wrought upon hundreds of us within the community, for dozens of years. His screams were a tribute to the memories of those he'd taken, those he'd harmed, and those who he protected so that they could take and harm as well.

I stepped outside to watch my work unfold. A small crowd of homeless folks gathered around me to watch the bigot burn. Even the lowest rungs of our society only has empathy for visible traumas. Mental breakdowns garner much attention, but little compassion.

More people began to gather. So as not to draw too much attention, I quickly used to Veil to mask myself as a fellow transient.

The few people who were close enough to witness the transformation blinked and did double-takes. They stared for a moment, but shrugged it off, thinking it had to be a mirage caused by either the severe cold, impressively high, blood alcohol levels, or both.

Like the Celeste persona, transient worked because it was also overlooked. My new persona was racially ambiguous, dressed in a tattered wool coat, with stringing white hair, and tobacco-stained teeth. A scraggly haired, filthily dressed vagrant wasn't as inconspicuous as a cute white woman, but in my present company, it provided instantaneous invisibility. At least, that's what I thought.

Three people to my right, I felt her piercing stare. Glancing over, my attention was immediately held captive by a woman who refused to break eye contact. Her thick black hair, was streaked with silver and tied back in a tight bun, revealing a strikingly slender face.

Her skin was tawny beige, and free from blemish. Her hollow green eyes sat sunken within their sockets, watching me with unblinking intensity. There were premature wrinkles on her hands and neck, their valleys and forks serving as an intricately complex, and wholly indecipherable schematic of a life spent surviving, as opposed to living. There was something about her, something more unsettling than the usual, standoffish, Minneapolitan look.

I put my head down and shuffled off into the night. I jogged a few blocks towards the stadium, rounded the corner, and headed South along the deserted, winter streets. Though I was more conspicuous now, there was a welcoming quiet that calmed my uneasy nerves.

The psychosomatic effects on the cop would stay in place indefinitely. His psyche was irrevocably scarred. In his mind, he would burn forever. Physical harm can be lasting sure, but it fades. And surface wounds can't hold a candle to psychological trauma. His remaining years would be permanently and irrevocably altered by those harrowing few minutes. He wouldn't be able to stay on the force, hell, he might not be able to stay out of an institution.

When I got to the end of the downtown area, I disengaged the Veil, and called for a rideshare. I smiled to myself while I waited. The streets were still frigid, but the sense of satisfaction warmed my vengeful heart. Demarcus wasn't the only one who demanded vengeance. There is much work to be done. Those who wouldn't or won't listen don't have to. They don't have to visualize or conceptualize.

They can see a concrete example of the solution.

The next morning, while checking the news, I read the follow up to the University's investigation of sexual assault allegations against the football team and numerous fraternities resulted in only lip service and faux compassion.

Last month they'd had a party where nine members of the team drugged and assaulted four women. Well, four women that came forward, the real number was undoubtedly much higher. University officials claimed that since they couldn't prove what had transpired at the party wasn't consensual, their hands were tied. Mine weren't. Since the administration was unwilling to give justice to the students who'd been violated, it was up to me.

Even though there were still some kinks to work out of the Veil technology- it had nearly slipped in the abrupt change from the blistering cold wind to the stale heat of the officer's car, after all- I couldn't let this injustice stand. I packed up my things, tweaked the settings on the Veil, and headed over to campus.

When I was eight years old, I had an idea. It was a viable solution to a problem that was mocked and rejected. It was the first of many ideas that were rejected and mocked by those lacking foresight. I've finally figured it out. The Veil enabled me to uncover the truth. In order to acquire vindication, demonstration always beats speculation.

ROD STRING NAIL CLOTH

THURSDAY ADDISON

I was born on the last day of the fourth month in the year 2180. My mother named me Thursday Addison, but six years ago, I became something more. I am not what I used to be. I was given a new designation, Angeli Iku. Loosely translated, it means angel of death. Considering my occupation, it's an apt moniker.

That's not tragic. That's sanctuary. Where I am currently is where I've always wanted to be. It's the only place I can accept being. What I am and what I will become is nothing other than what I was always meant to be. I cannot be more than what I do, when it's what I do that makes me what I am. But it's far more complicated than that. The slightest hint of devolution is my only fear. Though I'm comforted by my lack of both means and desire to regress, it's still an overwhelmingly ominous possibility.

Consider me an elasmobranch. Those fish with five to

seven gill slits and cartilaginous skeletons, like sharks and stingrays are my earthly brethren. I don't have gills or a cartilaginous skeleton. I don't have a skeleton at all really- not in the standard sense. The commonality with my oceanic siblings is metaphorical. It isn't a sameness of habitat or physicality, but rather serving as the constant target of deliberate and ignorant misconceptions.

People believe that all elasmobranchs must keep moving to survive. That's true for Mako and Whale sharks, who can only respire by swimming with mouths open to allow water to flow over their gills, it's not a blanket fact. Nurse sharks have muscles to draw the water in. Tiger sharks can do both. Just like people, they are far from monolithic.

Assumptions about me are similarly truncated. I have been called all manner of dysphemisms. I'm an abomination, an affront to both god and science. I'm a monster, a miracle, a mutation. I'm a glimpse at the next page in the story of humanity. I am all and more. I am nothing and less.

There was no way to misinterpret his howls of pain as anything other than anguish. His cries are reflexive. He can scream all he wants, but even he knows that he won't endure. There's no bargaining left. His remaining seconds were locked in stone. Death wasn't coming. It was here.

The introduction of a third is what breaks the binary.

There's a popular notion that life is either this or that. But once you realize the truth- that life is this, that, or a quadrillion other option- then you truly understand.

The only thing rarer than an actual either/or proposition, are people who know these instances are rare. But you shouldn't conflate improbable with impossible.

The hand on my shoulder is soft, but it bears an immeasurable weight. The tactile argument she presents is irrefutable. His physical distress is nothing compared to what she's passed on to me. The fact that she's chosen this move in particular, that she's chosen to use her rapidly diminishing energy reserves for an act of unfathomable mercy, obliterates and invalidates my convictions of justice.

I stopped cutting. A raging silence flooded the room. He'd lost consciousness, but he was breathing. The smell of his fear hung odorously in the space between the dingy, derelict walls. I looked up, my eyes overflowing with astonished admiration. First to the ceiling, searching for reason, but the slats above offered no decipherable explanation. I blinked and when my eyelids parted, found only her gaze. I dropped the bone saw, dropped to my knees, and let her drown in the welcoming folds of my blood-soaked arms.

Proselytes do not give much consideration to reason or evidence. They simply accept that what was, is not as such any longer. Life is a war of hours, yet I was planning the nanoseconds. I wasn't carrying a melee weapon to an artillery battle. I'd been screaming at nuclear bombardment.

No amount of amateur amputation would undo his atrocities. What was left of him, bound in that chair, leaking and spurting all over the dust-covered floor was completely neutralized. I pinned my marker on his chest and picked up his victim.

We exited through the doors into the freezing night air. Under the dim lights of the artificially clear sky, I listened as for the whirring of the transport siren. Within seconds, the heavily armored vehicle screeched to a halt, and took us back to the facilitation office.

My completion report was succinct, but detailed. The horrors I'd wrought upon him, would soon be shared with his co-conspirators. Forcing them to live through the trauma of intentional casualty, won't stop them, but it may help some reconsider their misguided motivations. I submitted documents and collected my wool. It wasn't much but it was enough to cover a maintenance installation.

I hadn't been under in months. My enhancements had performed, but it's always better to be over-equipped than find yourself lacking when you needed it most.

I checked in on the victim. There was a beauty in her, something irregular and compelling, that completely ensnared your attention. The scars and cuts had been treated. Her bones had been reset. She was whole again.

Within a few hours, nobody- herself included- would be able to tell what she'd been through. The horrors of her captivity and assault would be erased from her memory. The only evidence was contained in my report, and that would be locked within the archives, inaccessible and unavailable for review until a quarter century past her death.

I headed down the hall to the main roster. Though I've seen it almost daily for years, the twenty-foot tall, thirteen-sided obelisk of brass and mahogany was still breathtaking. I walked around to the side marked "A-B," entered my code. I looked up at my name, Thursday Addison, and watched the tiny, droplet-shaped bulb beneath "active" go out, while the bulb beneath "active" lit up.

I glanced at the clock. Ordinarily, after completing an assignment, I'd have the rest of the evening off, but it was still early, and with all the activity we'd been having lately, I was certain to get another job. There was enough time to run back to my quarters, grab a shower and make it to the central service area for maintenance installation.

The shower was tepid but sufficient. I toweled off and grabbed a fresh uniform. After making sure that the interlocking mesh of the cooling under-layer was taunt against my body, I stepped into the bio-sensor suit, and all-terrain boots. For personal style I wore my pleated skirt and tied my hair back into a high, tight ponytail.

When every buckle was secured, and every strap tightened, I donned my charcoal grey, ankle-length, flex-armor lined overcoat over my shoulders. I was barely three steps out of the door, when a young Blay-Jay noticed me.

"Thursday Addison?" He asked meekly.

"Yes, that's me, Blay-Jay." I nodded to confirm.

He looked so young. Even his uniform smelled brand new. I looked at my well-worn duty gear, and chuckled. Hard to believe how long it'd been since I was a cadet. Harder still to believe I'd ever been so fresh faced.

"I am Hammond, Abaeze Michael, Perennial Seraph cadet, Trans-Enclave Jurisdiction, bio-ID: Plus five, with a new assignment from the Governorship." He quickly bowed his head as a sign of respect, then handed me a Quarry scroll. I was about to open it, when I noticed him still standing there, waiting expectantly.

Back when I was a Blay-Jay, we were honored for the opportunity just to talk to a Greyjack. We wouldn't have taken payment if they'd offered. But that was a different time. I tossed him wool, and he scurried off with a smile.

I broke the seal, unrolled the parchment, and studied the overview details and objective criteria. There were reports of a massive disturbance near the Perennial Developments.

A lot of rescue and rebuild, but with heavy investigative and neutralization aspects. I wasn't too interested in making the trek all the out to the Perennial Developments, but the Governors were offering a tall stack of wool. The payout for expeditious completion was five times higher than usual.

I looked down at the response recommendations. The Governorship was recommending a team of four. That was security theater. The Perennial contained the Tithonus Courtyards, which were extremely affluent, so they wanted to put on a big show of force. I didn't need a team to give them a show. And besides, I didn't want to split the wool.

I tucked the parchment into my pocket and headed to the Central Service Area. I stopped by the Quadrupedal garage and signed out Kifo, marking a release time a few hours later. This would enable me to save time after the procedure. Descending the steps to the subterranean levels, I made my way to Dr. Riano's parlor, took my topicals without wincing, and reclined into the chair.

When the flesh of your head is pinned back exposing the facial muscles and bone, you need a distraction. I knew the procedure well. I'd gone through it a few times before. The implants and enhancements being applied to my Procerus, Orbicularis oculi, and Zygomaticus major muscles weren't just for fun, but that didn't make the procedure any less unsettling. As messy and gory as my assignments were, I don't think anyone has ever gotten used to seeing their own glistening red, bodily horrors reflected back to them in the vivid, visceral detail of all those shiny surfaces.

I felt around for the remote panel and turned up the volume on the broadcast. I loved listening to the news broadcasts while sitting in the chair. It was somewhat morbid sure, but the droning tones from the news readers had a calming effect on me. Even on days like today when it was nothing but a list of attacks and casualties, it was enough to redirect my focus. Some casualties stung more than others. Young residents were particularly painful. But in terms of fatalities on assignment? I've got zero sympathy for those who can't handle the hardware.

A careless Blay-Jay found themselves surrounded and began firing wildly, stopping only when their entire head caught fire. A lazy codger, too out of shape to give chase, cranks up the maximum discharge, expelling forty percent of their brain matter through the back of their head. A couple of freelancers build a ramshackle device that's nowhere near up to standards, only to see the flimsy components malfunction, resulting in subdermal decapitation and complete cranial liquefaction.

An unfocused mind was our greatest threat. Over the years, we'd lost good people due to nothing more than their own carelessness. These horror stories were the parables of the profession. This was the gospel according to Greyjacks. The central thesis running throughout every report is the inflexibly rigid confirmation that our rules weren't meant to be broken, bent, or even brushed against.

The regulations for a standard Ocular Unit aren't suggestions. Improper handling of your equipment results in gruesome death. Running the Oculars improperly heats up the charging chamber, which in turn overheats the conduction railings embedded along the nasal cavities and temporal bones of your skull. Prolonged exposure to what's essentially concentrated lightning isn't ideal. Unless you want your face to melt from the inside out, you follow every regulation no matter how seemingly redundant.

Riano sewed me up, applied the last liquid bandages, checked my sutures, and handed me a mirror. I caught look on his face as he was cleaning off his gloves. He was pleased with his work. I was pleased with his reaction. I've never known why my body adapts to the enhancements at a faster rate, but I'm damned glad it does. Those with rapid recovery after installation are at a significant advantage.

I listened intensely as he explained the guidelines for the new augmentations. The operating regulations were pretty much the same. When he was finished, I sat up in the chair and rubbed my neck. The Ocular upgrades were for efficiency and a smoother aesthetic. The raised ring around my right eye was a lot less prominent now.

I liked Riano. He's done all of my installations. He was the best because he was the most experienced, and he was the most experienced because he didn't care if you had the appropriate clearance, so long as you could pay. Sure, he's slightly unsanctioned, and somewhat unorthodox, but his licensing and permits were valid.

"Damn, Riano! Great work as always!" I mused, "I can barely see the sealing marks. Did you get a new technique?"

"Shucks, I'm just a humble bio-mechanic." He smiled, "But yes, that was a new technique. Some Blackjack cadets up for promotion were looking for an edge before exams."

"Wait, you did Ocular work on Blay-Jays?"

"Maybe it wasn't Blackjacks?" Riano coyly backpedaled, "I have so many clients, it's hard to keep them all straight."

"Riano, what would you do if they came for you?"

"What do you mean?" he feigned ignorance.

"You know what I mean. If the Governors found out you were giving Greyjack augmentations to Blay-Jays, they'd send a crew after you. Probably have me leading the raid."

"You want to know what I would do, if I found myself face to face with a bunch of Greyjacks and Aerostats, staring down the barrels of an assortment of steam canons and Oculars, many of which I installed myself?"

"Yeah," I chuckled, "What then?"

"I suppose, Miss Addison," he teased, knowing how much I hated being called Miss, "Should that day come, I'd leave a wealthy corpse... and you'd have to find someone else to do your enhancements."

"Well, let's hope that day never comes then."

"For you as well." he arched an eyebrow.

"What do you mean by that?" I asked.

"Come on Thursday, it's not like you're a stranger to bending the rules."

"That's a pretty heavy accusation to throw."

"Not an accusation. Just an observation. Your last assignment, wasn't the recommended response team supposed to be comprised of two Greyjacks?"

"Yes, but I got the job done by myself."

"And what about the next assignment, hm? I noticed the parchment tucked into your coat pocket. How many Greyjacks is it recommending?"

"Like I said, I can get the job done." I retorted.

"Oh, there's no question about that." Riano shrugged, "You always do, but I was under the impression that when the Governorship recommends something, it's best to take them up on it."

"Maybe for the other Greyjacks, but with my skills, recommendations are just recommendations. And besides, following the recommendations aren't a law. They're more like a custom."

"Customs are there for a reason. I just worry about you getting into something you can't get out of."

"Aw Riano," I chuckled, "How sentimental. Here I thought I was just another customer."

"A frequent and high paying one." Riano scoffed, "Speaking of which, I trust you've got the wool for this?"

"Always. What's the damage?"

"Eleven." I climbed off the table and paid him.

I looked in the mirror again. A pale scar began just below my cheek, ran up the side of my face and disappeared beneath my hairline. It was long and large, but within a few days, it would be completely healed.

As I slipped into my overcoat, my Angelfire shifted. I adjusted it, as Riano bristled at the sight of the firearm.

"Hey, Thursday."

"Yes, Riano."

"You've got top of the line Oculars. Doesn't an Angelfire seem a bit redundant? I'm expecting some new dueling edges to arrive by the end of next week, if you ever change your mind about that gun of yours." he winced.

"No thanks, Riano," I smiled, "I like a pair of edges as much as anyone, but I'll stick to my Angelfire."

"Indeed." Riano conceded, "Just though I'd ask.

Especially with you doing assignments solo, dueling edges could be essential tools in your arsenal."

"In the rare case that something gets past the Oculars, the Angelfire puts to rest. Not to mention I've got Kifo."

"I mean, it's dangerous out there. Squirrels are getting more and more brazen."

"I took out my last assignment with a bone saw. Didn't even need to use my firepower. Don't get me wrong, I like to be equipped, but I think a pair of mind-controlled, flying knives orbiting around me would be overkill."

"If you're sure, I mean I can—"

"Good to see you again, Riano. To life." I cut him off.

"To life." he nodded, returning the farewell sentiment, his shoulders dropping with disappointment.

I gave him a friendly pat on the shoulder and left. I headed back to the Quadrupedal garage, took Kifo out into the lobby and started her internal engines. As she whirred to life, I stroked her sleek body. Her primary chassis was newly accentuated by a few cobalt blue stripes of velvet. The embellishment was gauche, but I'd done well on the last few assignments, so with the extra wool in my pockets, so I figured why not.

She seemed to quiver with anticipation as her computational devices began making their initial assessments. I absolutely loathed shutting her off, but it was standard procedure when visiting the Central Service Area.

Personally, I felt that the Governors were far too furtive when it came to the installation of new implants or components. But I also understood why they didn't like to have our huge, clockwork dogs sniffing around the critical inner workings of the Enclave, logging billions of intimate details into their data recorders.

I inserted the assignment parchment into Kifo's receptor slot. The electronic light on the back of her head blinked to confirm receipt, and subsequent incineration. I set her to transport mode. Her legs retracted into her body and the vector field posts at her shoulder joints lit up. I mounted her, locked my bootheels in place, and set the velocity max of 400. When we got to cruising altitude, I took a nap. We when arrived the next morning, there was no need to reconfirm the location. The carnage was astounding.

Hundreds of thousands of the injured and the dead were scattered about the smoldering remains. I could hardly believe that the Squirrels were capable of this much horror. The Squirrels were menacing and loathsome, but they tended to stick to minor infractions. Enclave destruction and residential death at this scale was unprecedented.

Kifo touched down by the perimeter. I jumped off her back and sent her off to scan the area. I probably should've stayed with her, but the assignment gets done faster when she's able to hunt freely. I know she's just a complicated contraption full of biotic mechanisms, electrical components, and propellant engines, but that complicated contraption absolutely loves to hunt.

Over the next few hours, I assisted where I could; helping survivors tend to their wounds, sort through their heirlooms, and identify and incinerate their dead.

When night fell, I went on patrol with Kifo, searching for clues as to what equipment the Squirrels had newly acquired that enabled them to enact such absolute ruination.

We made it to the Eos River that ran along the back of the Tithonus Courtyards. The Eos is a photonic tributary that flowed through the Enclave. Access to the thirty-foot wide stream of pulchritudinous light was heavily restricted, including the few dozen feet of spectacular brilliance that curved gently along the southern edge of the courtyards.

If it weren't clear from the names, the founders of our Enclave were unabashed Hellenophiles. Eos was named for the Greek Goddess of the Dawn, the daughter of Hyperion and Theia. Hyperion was a Titan, known as the Bringer of Light, who travels high above the Earth. Theia was also a Titan, known as the divine, eldest daughter or Gaia.

Despite the occasional, insignificant complaints at community gatherings, it was easy to see why Tithonus was off-limits to anyone with an augmented bio-ID ranked below fifty-one percent. You couldn't have some majority organic messing around in here. Inevitably, they'd ruin it, just like our ancestors had done ages ago.

Even with my numerous components, there are thousands of areas in the Enclave that are prohibited unless I'm on assignment. For a Greyjack like me who'd had a lot of augmentations, I fully understood the reason why we enhance. I paused for a moment to enjoy the view. I don't get a lot of leisure time, and even when I do, it's not often I get to visit Tithonus, but I absolutely love it here.

I'm not a Squirrel. I respect the boundaries. As a cadet, I couldn't wait to get my first augment. I squealed like a child after dumping those disgusting, carbon dioxide spewing natural lungs, and replacing them with a set of emission free Oxygenators. And anyone who says they prefer a gastrointestinal tract to protein and nutrient infusers is either lying or insane.

Sometimes, not often, but sometimes, there's a tiny voice that pops up in the back of my mind, telling me how great it would be to one day smell the lush trees and supple grass, to truly experience this sanctuary, rather than rely on the data from my olfactory sensors to inform me about it.

Every time that traitorous little voice pops up, I immediately silence it, by looking at the exterior monitors. The reason why the environment outside the Enclave was uninhabitable was because of that type of thinking.

Places like these are a glorious reminder of why the laws we have and uphold were established in the first place. The natural combinations of color, texture, and scent were an unparalleled sensory gift. Why spoil that with the imperfect?

I continued walking along the river. I kept my Oculars armed. Just because Squirrels were ignorant didn't mean they weren't dangerous. A few hundred feet later, I came to a clearing of artificial trees, and sure enough, I spotted one.

She had fair skin and closely cropped, platinum hair, but she was surprisingly tall and muscular. Squirrels tended to be borderline emaciated- but this one was impressively fit.

She was huddled, in the middle of the grass and stared up at me with her glossy, dilated eyes. She was looking in my direction but seemed completely unfazed. I flashed a few sparks from my Ocular, as a diversion, so she wouldn't notice that I'd un-clipped the Angelfire from my belt.

I'd been a Greyjack long enough to spot a trap, but if there were other Squirrels hiding in the tree-line, they wouldn't be able to reach me before I decimated this well-built piece of bait. Even if they gave up their position early, I had plenty of time and space to neutralize any threat.

She put her head down. I quickly checked my peripherals to make sure there weren't any additional Squirrels looking to flank me. In that split second that I took my eyes off her, she jumped to her feet and began closing the gap between us. It was clear that she had been doping, but even for a Squirrel hopped up on whichever pharmaceuticals were popular with them these days, her speed and agility were shockingly fast. Steadying my aim, I fired.

It was a direct hit. Taking hit from an Ocular blast is usually a civilizer. Doesn't matter what your minimum augment percentage was, having a slug of concentrated energy tear through you with a dozen megajoules of kinetic force calms you down. But she was still coming.

She should've been screaming in agony, writhing around on the dirt, grasping desperately at the smoldering, cauterized hole where the entire left side of her upper torso used to be. Instead, she took the full brunt of the blast without a scratch. I kept my composure, lined up another shot, and fired again. Nothing.

She must have ingested an entire medicine cabinet full of incredibly strong pharmaceuticals. I fired again. Nothing. I fired again. Nothing. She kept closing the distance between us. Steadily. Methodically. Rapidly.

I alternated between my Ocular and Angelfire, precisely firing in deliberate, calculated bursts. I carefully aimed at strategic points on her anatomy. Every shot selected for maximum damage. Every shot hit directly where targeted. Every shot was ineffectual. She kept coming.

I could feel my Ocular beginning to overheat. I made one last attempt at annihilation, letting off a quintet of shots into the center of her emotionless face.

It had no effect.

She shoved me to the ground, pinning my arms with her knees. I could feel her warm breath on the tip of my nose as her eyes drilled fiery holes into my own. I dug my heels into the ground and rolled my hips, but I couldn't to gain leverage to topple her.

My earlier barrage hadn't slowed this monstrously powerful Squirrel, but at point blank, it might've had enough kick to push her off, and buy me some time. I wiggled for position and stretched out my arms, but my Angelfire was just out of reach.

She exhaled slowly and opened her eyes. She reached up with both of her dirty hands and grabbed her stringy, platinum hair above her ears. Slowly, she began to pull. All I could do was stare as she drizzled ragged handfuls of her platinum locks over my chest and face.

She reached around to the back of her head, firmly gripping her hair at the root. Her mouth turned slightly upward. It was barely perceivable, but she was definitely smiling as she pulled the flesh right off of her head. Through the crimson mask, her eyes glowed bright yellow, crackling with static and smoke. This wasn't a power display or intimidation tactic. This was an introduction. She wanted me to know that she wasn't scared. She wanted me to know exactly what I was dealing with.

Her bio-ID had to have exceeded 100%. In all my years as a Greyjack, I'd only ever heard reports of people enhancing their bio-IDs of this level. Their bodies had gone as far as the astounding innovations and near-nonexistent boundaries of contemporary medicine could take them, so instead of boosting the old, they replaced with the new.

The reports were all observational though. The subjects they detailed were never considered dangerous. It makes sense. When you had the kind of money to render yourself medically immortal, you don't waste time on pedestrian trivialities like violence.

There were rumors that in the early days of the Enclave, that Aaron Harvey, the scientist who had created the deity-defying breakthroughs, abducted students to use in clandestine experiments. Harvey had cured death, now his sights were set something more.

Sure, Harvey was a real person. He was a brilliant, though tragic contemporary of Lavell Douglas. His work on augmentations were the foundation for many procedures we still have now. He'd ultimately deemed his work a failure, because he couldn't save his wife, and wound up killing all of his test subjects, and eventually, himself. But the rest of it was just nonsense we used to spook Blay-Jays.

Squirrels didn't have means to render themselves 100% augmented. Even if they did manage to find it, they would never use it. Like other degenerate luddites throughout history who clung to their regressive philosophies, they were too sanctimonious see that their collective idiocy and technological abstinence set them at a huge disadvantage. This Squirrel however, was clearly an outlier.

I didn't see the strike. I felt it shatter my sternum. The augments installed in me effectively killed the nerves so there wasn't any pain. She was fast and she was accurate. Before I could raise my arms or charge my Ocular, she'd disabled the primary drivers that enhanced my skeletal frame. Without that augmentation, I was paralyzed.

I couldn't turn my head, but out of the corner of my eye, I saw Kifo lunge at the Squirrel. The Squirrel caught Kifo by the neck with one hand and grabbed Kifo's lower jaw with the other. With brutal efficiency, she tore Kifo's head in two, showering me with mechanical innards. The Squirrel dangled the headless body like a trinket. She examined the permanently inoperable chassis for a few moments, then returned her gaze to me.

With a skinless smirk, she effortlessly tossed Kifo's remains aside. I braced myself as the Squirrel reared back, her mouth agape, her fists raised menacingly over her head.

My demise was abruptly interrupted by a flash that shone brighter than unfiltered sunlight through a magnification lens. The Squirrel screamed and jumped off me, dashing angrily towards the source of the brilliant flash. Squinting, I could just make out a silhouette in the midst of the illuminance. The details of the figure blurred with the colors and sounds around me, as my eyes tried to adjust.

In the midst of the maelstrom, the silhouetted figure grew sharper and more define as it emerged from the storm. The Squirrel lunged at the silhouette with a horrific scream. The silhouette caught her and tore her in half in the same way that the Squirrel had caught and destroyed Kifo. The Squirrel's innards arced over the silhouetted figure like a macabre halo of fluids and bone fragments, shredded tissue and intestinal debris.

The newly bisected Squirrel's parts landed with a sickening thud on opposites sides of the silhouetted figure. The Squirrel's separated legs kept kicked uselessly on the ground, while the upper half of the Squirrel's torso kept clawing at the figure, her skinless face twisted into a macabre mask of feral rage.

The figure looked down at relentless torso and stomped on the Squirrel's head repeatedly until there was nothing left but a jagged mass of crushed bone, glowing augment circuitry, and bluish-gray brain matter, pouring out of the ragged neck like a cornucopia of visceral horror.

The figure came towards me, stepping over the Squirrel's now headless torso, that lay still in a sticky, damp puddle of cerebral fluid. The figure examined me for a few moments, then reached down into the cavity where that Squirrel had disabled my primary drivers and began deftly rummaging around, rewiring, reconnecting, repairing.

Although our proximity now allowed me to make out facial features, and my memory augments enabled me to retain tens of billions of details about hundreds of billions of data points, I couldn't identify her.

Her pupil-less eyes were matte grey and unreflective. She had the eyes of a corpse. She never blinked, but that wasn't what made them disturbing. They were like the sky outside the walls of the Enclave, as unyieldingly vast and endless as the depths of space.

Her expression was devoid of any semblance of life. The most distinctive feature was an intricate, twisting pattern embedded all over the impossibly smooth, honey brown flesh of her face. The pattern glowed slightly lighter than her skin, as though her veins were filled with liquid light.

I was transfixed, but even more so, I was confused. Markings so prominently displayed on the face, should've made this person instantly, irrefutably recognizable, but they didn't trigger any matches in my residential logs. Her bio-

ID didn't register or set off any notification alarms.

She finished the last of my reconnections, and I felt my mobility return. I immediately rolled over and grabbed Angelfire, aiming it unsteadily between her mesmerizingly monochromatic eyes.

"Really?" she smirked, smacking Angelfire out her face, and nearly out of my hand, "You think I'm a threat? If I was, I wouldn't have repaired you. I would've ended you."

Wow, she was strong. Assuming she was from some elite Aerostat division, I identified myself formally.

"Apologies. I'm Addison, Thursday Juliana, Perennial Seraph with Universal Trans-Enclave Jurisdiction, and Quadruped Accompanied. My bio-ID is Plus Eighty. Designation, Angeli Iku."

"Yeah, I figured." she stared at me eyebrow, "Can't believe you engaged with those rudimentary enhancements.

"Rudimentary?" I cried, "I just had enhancement implanted earlier this week!"

"And how'd that work out for you?" she spat.

"Fair point." I conceded, "But still, how were you able to neutralize that Squirrel?"

"It wasn't just a Squirrel." she scolded, "That was an Apogee. You see, Thursday, there's a reason why we recommended a quartet of Greyjacks."

"Wait a minute. How would you know the response

recommendations? Unless…" I scanned her bio-ID again, "That's why you're not triggering any matches in my residential logs. You're a member of the Governorship! And your bio-ID doesn't register because it's outside the scope of my parameters!"

"My status is unimportant. What matters is that I was here, before the Apogee neutralized you. You're an effective Greyjack, but your hubris is hazardous. You have the skill. You have the equipment. But the most powerful weapons are rendered useless in the face of wisdom and strategy."

"I understand."

"I hope so, Thursday. I hope so. To life."

"To life."

She nodded goodbye. As she took a few steps back towards the tree line, she began to glow, enveloping the clearing in the same electrifying illumination that had appeared when she did. Seconds later, the light vanished. I found myself standing alone, with the broken remains of Kifo, and the twitching corpse of the Squirrel at my feet.

ROD STRING NAIL CLOTH

ROD STRING NAIL CLOTH

THE HESITANT ENVOY

"Oh my god, what's going on!"

"Don't be afraid, I'm here to help."

"Where is everyone?"

"They're all still here, you just can't see them. And besides, it's where we are that counts."

"So... where are we?"

"It's very complex."

"Try me."

"Let's see. What's the best way that I could phrase this for you? We're in a... moment."

"A moment?"

"Yes, a moment."

"I don't...what do you mean, a moment?"

"I told you. It's very complex."

"Yeah, I guess. A moment?"

"Okay, moving on. The reason for our conversation, is that you've been randomly selected to—"

"I'm sorry. I can't stop thinking about what you said?"

"What I've just said? Well, I've just said it so..."

"No, no. Not what you just said, what you said before, about us being in a... moment?"

"Oh, that again?"

"Yes, if you wouldn't mind elaborating..."

"All right. What you refer to as the passage of time, is really just a subjective perspective based on your remarkably miniscule observational capabilities, and the technology that I'm currently using exists outside of those remarkably miniscule observational capabilities, and as such I am able to work around the quadri-dimensional aspects of your conceptual viewpoints, removing you from your truncated, trifurcated notions of space, and your woefully inaccurate, observed singular dimension of time and relativistic effects of where and when, but for sake of your sanity, still tethered you to a fixed reference point. In this instance, these seats, at this table, at this cafe) allowing your physical quantities to travel and transcend some incomprehensible distances relative to that reference point. You are both here and there, because in order to be here, you need a there, in order for you to leave it and be here, even though you're still there, because there only is there because you are here."

"So, we're in... a moment?"

"Precisely. May we move on?"

"Yes."

"You've been randomly selected to speak on behalf of humanity. Now, I was able to convince my superiors from moving forward with the obliteration of your species, on the condition that any one of you humans, as you call yourselves, could provide a sufficient argument for the continuation of your species."

"Wow."

"Wow?"

"Yeah. Wow."

"I'm sorry, I've just informed you that your species, homo-sapiens, human beings, you will all be destroyed unless you can give me a reason to spare you, that I can take back to my superiors, and all you can say is...wow?"

"How about...whoa?"

"Whoa?"

"Yes, it's like wow, but with different letters."

"You're not taking this seriously."

"Oh, I am. I just don't know if it's worth it."

"Hold on. You don't know if what is worth it? Are you saying you don't know if it's worth it to...save humanity?"

"Yeah, that's a tough one."

"Is it, though?"

"Actually, yes."

"You understand I'm talking about the complete decimation of everyone and everything you know- including yourself. There'd be no more humans- at all."

"No, I get that, but..."

"You're still not sure?"

"Exactly."

"Wow."

"See, you get it now, huh?"

"I just don't understand. This has been the standard procedure for every planet we've encountered since we began our interstellar audit. We monitor the dominant lifeform on a world, and grade it based on a number of factors. If the result is less that sufficient, we select an envoy to represent the species and speak on their behalf."

"And how has that worked out for other planets?"

"Pretty well actually. I mean, our intention isn't to destroy all intelligent life. Ideally, every planet would make the grade and we wouldn't have to select an envoy at all. But even on those occasions, usually the envoy is successful."

"That's impressive."

"It really is. Most lifeforms when faced with complete annihilation tend to get their act together so to speak. And the best part, is that there's rarely any recidivism."

"Rarely?"

"Well, you know. You do what you can. Gliese did a complete overhaul. That little exoplanet was right on the brink, but when we paid them a visit, and explained what would happen if they didn't straighten up, they got it together quickly."

"Gliese?"

"It's an exoplanet about 22 light years away from here. They were in really bad shape, let me tell you. You know how you Earthlings are still obsessed with maintaining borders and fighting amongst yourselves for resources and greed, and all that? Before we got there, Gliese made Earth look like Quokvhaad."

"Quokvhaad?"

"Oh, that's right. I keep forgetting the limitations of human knowledge."

"Sorry."

"Oh, it's not your fault. Quokvhaad is a star in the Centaurus Galaxy. The dominant lifeforms, the Oskalesha, have maintained a perfect record since the dawn of their civilization. I mean, they're just spectacular little beings."

"And Gliese was so bad, it made us look perfect?"

"You humans are absolute trash, but the Gliese are on another level. But then we made a visit. Their envoy pleaded the case, and in the time since, they've become exemplary. Just a model example of a bad planet made good."

"But you did say rarely any recidivism."

"Yes…"

"Rarely doesn't mean never."

"Mars."

"No, rarely doesn't mean Mars either."

"No, I mean Mars is an example of recidivism. We'd had high hopes for your neighbors. But after repeated visits, finally, we had to pull the plug, as the saying goes."

"So, there's life on Mars!"

"There was. Past tense. It was a lot like Earth. But unfortunately, they didn't listen. It's a shame too. They had a great music scene. But I'm getting off topic. Surely you now understand what's at stake, so are you ready to argue on behalf of all humanity?"

"Yeah, I've got nothing for you."

"What do you mean?"

"I mean, if you need someone to defend humans, I'm not the one to do it."

"You realize that you're human too, yes?"

"Yes, of course."

"And you realize that by not serving as the envoy, that you, along with every other living thing on the planet will be eradicated. No exceptions. You'll be completely wiped from existence. Your planet will look like Mars."

"Got it."

"Yet you still can't think of a single thing to say in humanity's defense? There's nothing that your species is good at? There's nothing worth saving?"

"Well…"

"Go on."

"If I had to choose something, I think uh…"

"Yes, yes…"

"We're good at…ignorance."

"Good at ignorance?"

"Yeah…ignorance."

"That's not really what we're looking for."

"It's probably what we're best at."

"I am a physical manifestation of an intergalactic intelligence tasked with auditing life across the entire multiverse. We assess every planet, and when it falls short, we offer a chance for the dominant species to redeem itself. And even in the face of extinction, you can't think of a single reason why your species- your world should be spared?"

"Not really."

"Not really?!"

"Okay, like, what if we spared some people, but not like, all the people? Is that an option?"

"I'd have to check. I think there have been a few cases like that, but the circumstances were really extenuating."

"That's fair. So how long do you need?"

"Done."

"That was fast."

"Not really, but I can see how you'd think it was."

"I'm not sure if that was an insult, but even if it was, I'm not sure if I should be offended."

"It wasn't, but you still should be."

"Ah, I see."

"Anyway, yes. If you can provide criteria for determining who should be spared, and who should be removed, we can accommodate that request, and suspend annihilation.

"Well that's great!"

"Okay then, so who's getting removed?"

"Um, well, let's see. I suppose we can start with the all the racists and bigots."

"But wait, aren't all people a bit racist?"

"No. That's just something that racist people say so that they don't have to feel bad about being racist."

"Got it. Okay, they're gone. Anyone else?"

"Well, I suppose with no racists or bigots, we can also get rid of homophobes, and transphobes."

"I'd already classified them as bigots."

"Thanks! This is a lot easier than I thought it'd be."

"No reason to make it challenging. It's just the fate of your species and planet, is all."

"Right. No biggie."

"Anyone else?"

"Misogynists, chauvinists, and incels."

"Good call. Phew, those incels, huh? They're a baffling lot. They hate women, but also are obsessed with women."

"Yeah, not the sharpest tools in the candy dish. Speaking of which, what about the proudly stupid?"

"Proudly stupid?"

"Like the people who know they don't know much of anything but are super proud of that fact."

"That's a really big chunk of your home country."

"Yeah, unfortunately."

"This is a solid list. Very comprehensive. Now--"

"Theocrats."

"Theocrats?"

"Theocrats. Y'know. Religious zealots."

"Oh sure."

"I've got nothing against religious or spiritual people, but the theocratic zealots? Yeah, be a much better world without them on it."

"So that's racists and bigots, including homophobes and transphobes, misogynists, chauvinists, incels, the proudly stupid, and theocrats."

"It's a good list, yeah?"

"Really solid."

"Thank you."

"I'll take this back to my superiors and—"

"Ooh, almost forgot, corrupt people, greedy people, sanctimonious people, and physically abusive people."

"Look, I've got to level with you. I know that this is a list of the worst traits of the worst people, and you're undoubtedly drawing from personal experience to curate this list, but it's not just your comparatively narrow window that's full of these kinds of folks."

"How full are we talking?"

"Let me see, tallying up the results here…of the nine billion humans on this planet, after removing those with these traits…forty-two million."

"Worldwide?"

"Yes."

"Wow."

"I know, right?"

"I didn't realize it'd be that many."

"Jeez, you're really not a glass half-full type, huh?"

"I know people."

"Sadly, it seems you do. Well, I suppose I should make preparations. Removing eight point nine-five-eight billion people is a big job."

"I suppose it is."

"This has been…"

"Fun."

"Not particularly, no."

"That's fair. Can I ask you a question before you go?"

"Sure."

"How are you going to do it?"

"Come again?"

"Annihilating eight point nine-five-eight billion people. How are you going to do it?"

"Oh, I'm not going to do it. That's insane."

"What? Then who is?"

"You are."

"Me!"

"Of course. We'll provide you with a few super weapons, a map, and a list."

"I don't want to kill anyone."

"You just gave me a list of literally billions of people you want dead."

"Yeah but, I don't want to kill them, myself."

"Let me get this straight, you want these people dead, but you don't want to make them dead?"

"Precisely."

"You don't think that's more a bit contradictory?"

"How so?"

"So, it's fine as long as it's a physical manifestation of an intergalactic intelligence tasked with auditing life across the entire multiverse. But you're too good for the work?"

"I mean, I'm not too good for it. I suppose I'm not too bad for it either. Either way, I'm just not the killing type."

"Go back a few pages, and there's a pretty significant chunk of the conversation that says otherwise."

"What are you talking about, pages?"

"Oh, that's right, fourth wall breaking is outside your scope of perception."

"Fourth wall? There aren't any walls. We're sitting at a table outside this café."

"Sure, we are."

"Wait, so when you say fourth wall, do you mean like on a television show or movie when the actor looks at the camera and talks directly to the audience?"

"Television show, movies, plays, it's also done in literature too, y'know."

"Yeah I know. I read. So, none of this is real? This is all just some form of entertainment for a cosmic audience?"

"If you can never verify it one way or the other, does the answer to that really matter?"

"Wow, that's...that's astonishingly deep."

"Thank you."

"So, what do I do now?"

"Well, I can provide you with the means to kill eight point nine-five-eight billion people, or you can give me a reason to spare humanity."

"I uh…I guess the latter. Let's save humanity."

"Okay then. Why?"

"Well I mean, because we don't know why we're all here. We might be just a planetary entertainment program, maybe we're not, but maybe I can get enough folks to realize that this may all be for nothing, and as such it could be taken away in an nanosecond, everything and everyone might be gone just like that, without a second thought, that given the chance, perhaps we can make things right."

"That's a good answer. Humanity will be spared."

"Wait, can we still get rid of the first part of my list?"

"The racists and bigots, including homophobes and transphobes, misogynists, chauvinists, incels, the proudly stupid, and theocrats?"

"Yeah, just them. Like, could you do that?"

"You know what, why not. I suppose we could help you out just this once."

"Thanks!"

"No problem. Can't have all these shorts ending ambiguously. Nice to have a happy ending."

"What?"

"Never mind."

ROD STRING NAIL CLOTH

THE LYDIAN MODE

Contrary to what a lot of movies and television shows would have you believe; the men's restroom isn't some morose sanctuary of masculine silence. On the contrary, guys are just as chatty as the stereotypical depictions of our counterparts in the other bathroom.

Men give pep talks asking how many open buttons they can pull off. They monopolize the mirrors and make temporary friends with strangers. But don't dismiss all the preening, chuckling, chatting, and adjusting as flights of camaraderie filtered through the prismatic lens of metropolitan vanity. The bathroom is serious business.

"Sorry I'm late, Evan. I'd told Jay on the phone that the train was due in ten minutes, didn't realize he'd told everyone I'd be here in five." Darnel shook his hand.

"Good to see you, Darnel, glad you could make it."

It had been ages since we'd shared a stage together, and I was excited to perform with him again.

"Seriously man, sorry."

"No worries!" Evan chuckled, smoothing the same waft of hair over and over, trying to get it to sit just right. "I'm still fixing my 'do."

"What's with White guys and their hair?" Darnel asked.

"Got to look full man." Evan smirked.

"I can see that. Hey, maybe I should run out and tell them we need an extra thirty-forty minutes?" Darnel teased.

"Dude, chill." Evan feigned offence, "You're telling me that you don't ever worry about losing your hair?"

"No, not really man. It's like you white fellas are scared or something. What's the worst that could happen? Oh no, I'm bald now. Oooh. Scary."

"It's about style, man. I'm not scared."

"Dude, you white guys are totally scared. That's why so many of you start sporting that weird sort of donut look."

"Donut look?"

"Hair on the sides and back, bald circle on top."

"Ah yes. Lot of guys sporting that look."

"I mean, it's not so bad, when they keep what's left trim, but some of you white cats?"

"What do we do?" Evan snorted.

"You white cats- well some of you- you grow it super long on the sides just makes it way more obvious that there's nothing on the top. You never see Black guys worrying about it or trying to grow a side-fro."

"No man, you're wrong. I've seen thousands of Black guys with that look."

"Thousands?" Darnel laughed, "You've seen thousands of Black men with a donut? Really? Thousands?"

"Okay, not thousands, but like…more than a few."

"Bet you twenty dollars, it's less than ten."

"Hey, we've got to look our best. I need every single follicle. Can't risk looking like a hair metal singer from an eighties music video."

"I'm just saying. You look sharp."

"We both do."

"Exactly. And nobody is going to mistake you for Axl Rose or David Lee Roth or something. And even if they do, that still works…on the older women."

"Aw, what?" Evan teased, "You don't like it when they've got a few miles on the meter?"

"I mean, I like age on a woman." Darnel shot back defensively, "It's sexy. Hell, Zola has got about the better part of a decade over me. But it'd be nice if just for once, I could chat up someone closer who closer to my age group than my mom's."

"Maybe it's that sweet porkpie hat." Evan playfully tapped the brim of Darnel's hat, "Reminds them of their college years back in the 1950s. Drives them wild!"

"Hey!" Darnel barked and re-adjusted the hat, so it sat just right. "The 1950s? How old do you think I'm talking?"

"I don't know. Old." Evan laughed.

"Okay, but not that old," Darnel chuckled, "Anyway. I didn't get a set list. I haven't played with you guys in a while, but I'm sure I can pick it up."

"Oh, wow man," Evan glanced over and looked at Darnel's guitar case, "Didn't Jay tell you?"

"Tell me what?"

"Don't need you to play on this."

"I'm confused. Jay said you needed me to sit in."

"Yeah man, we're doing a few old school rap covers. Needed some color on the stage, if you know what I mean."

"What the hell?" Darnel spat.

"We tried some rap tunes last few gigs, and they went over really well, but…" Evan smoothed his collar arrogantly, "Look, I'll be straight with you. A bunch of white guys doing some rap tunes don't have the same impact on the audience. We get you on stage with us, that adds some legitimacy, you know what I'm saying?"

"How exactly would I add legitimacy?"

"Dude." Evan sighed.

"What?" Darnel frowned, feeling the sickening combination of offense and agitation welling up in his gut.

"Look," Evan demurred, "you're the only Black guitarist I know well enough to call up for a gig like this."

"But see," now Darnel was pissed, "That's just it. I'm a Black guitarist. Guitarist. Not a rapper. What the hell man, when we first met, you knew I was in school getting my degree in jazz studies."

"Come on man," Evan rubbed the bridge of his nose, "It's just rap. You can put aside the jazz snobbery for a couple sets, right?"

"This isn't snobbery!" Darnel yelled, "You want me to jump on stage and be your token? Be the dancing darkie hype-man for a bunch of suburban boys pretending to rap? I'm a true musician, man! I'm glad you paid me up front."

"Hey!" Evan stopped preening and frowned at me, "It's the peak of Saturday night. Those folks don't want a musical history lesson. That crowd only wants to do four things. They want to drink and dance, and then dance and drink. And they aren't going to do that to a bunch of jazz standards you hear in a dental office. And if they see a black face on that stage, they'll go nuts! Which means more gigs, which means more money- for all of us."

"Don't call me again." Darnel bit his lip, barely containing his rage.

"Really man? It's like that?!" Evan shrieked.

"That's how you made it." Darnel held firm, "I'm a true musician. Just even asking me…. even thinking that I would consider doing something like this—"

"Okay then." Evan interrupted dismissively, "Good luck trying to pack a house with that waiting room music."

Evan scoffed and stormed out of the bathroom. Darnel looked at his reflection, angry at the face staring back at him. It was disappointed and furious, but relieved.

He turned on the faucet and rinsed off his face, then looked in the mirror again. For a split second, he caught myself thinking that maybe he could've said 'screw it,' and just goofed around, doing few hip hop tunes with the band. He shook that notion right out of his head. He'd had a hard-enough time finding gigs as it was. He wasn't about to exploit himself like that. Weaving his way through the crowd, he looked back at the stage.

"How's everyone doing tonight?" Evan yelled into the mic, "Before we get started, I just want to give a quick shout out, and give it up for a *true musician*, Darnel Lexington! Unfortunately, Darnel Lexington can't join us tonight, because Darnel Lexington is just way too good for this kind of stage. He told me so himself. But I just want to let Darnel Lexington know that there's no hard feelings, and if he'd ever consider slumming it, we'd love to have him!"

Evan smirked at Darnel from center stage. It was a beautifully devious hit. Even if the booking agent wasn't there, the waitstaff, bartenders, sound techs, and bouncers all were. And having the headlining act call out someone by name wouldn't go unnoticed. However slim the chances Darnel may have had getting a gig at the venue before, they were next to nothing now.

The rest of the group exchanged mocking looks. Through the scattered drunken applause and jeers, Darnel shot daggers at Evan and the band, allowing the warm rush of hatred to wash over him. He grabbed an empty beer bottle from the bar. Darnel felt the smooth glass in his palm. He knew it was a horrible idea but knew that he was going to do it anyway.

The amber glass arced gracefully over the crowd, shattering on the stage. Evan screamed and dropped the microphone. The bouncers pounced on Darnel, picked him up, and literally threw him out of the bar.

The sidewalk was packed. Darnel dusted himself off. The only thing that was really hurt was his pride. He picked up his guitar case and dusted it off, ignoring the snickering kids holding cellphones and whispering. A terribly whitewashed rendition of Kendrick Lamar blared through the closed doors of the bar. The crowd inside squealed with glee and began bobbing and awkwardly gyrating.

Darnel shook his head and wandered down the crowded sidewalk. The air was charged with the distinctive energy that can only come from the electrifying combination of warm weather, copious amounts of alcohol, and youthful indiscretions. While waiting at the crosswalk he felt his pocket vibrate. He pulled out his phone and glanced at the caller ID. It was his girlfriend, Zola. He stepped back from the curb, took the call.

"Hey Zola, what's up? Everything okay?"

"Oh good. You picked up." her voice was flat.

"Of course, I picked up, everything all right?"

"I was going to leave a message, but I'm glad that I don't have to. Better to do this one on one."

"Do what? What's going on?"

"You want to explain to me why when I got home, the fridge is empty, and the mail is still on the counter?" her voice was no longer flat, it was drenched in fury.

"Oh shoot. I'm sorry."

"You left me a message said you didn't get the call for the gig until six. You were here all day, and in all that time, you couldn't take a half hour to pick up groceries and drop off the mail?"

"I'm sorry. I was rehearsing, and then when I got the call for the gig, I completely forgot about it."

"If it was such an important gig, then why aren't you playing now? "You know what, it doesn't matter. I'm done."

"What do you mean, you're done?"

"Exactly what I said. Pick up your stuff tomorrow."

"But—"

"It's been over a year. Your music isn't going anywhere, and I'm too old to wait any more. I'm done." She hung up.

Darnel was out of a gig, out of a relationship, and out of options. He was crushed, but at least he still had his guitar. He put his phone away and looked around. It was a gorgeous night. The kind of night that could only be truly felt by the overlooked and dejected. Darnel didn't have a stage to play. He didn't have an apartment to go home to. But he could still make music.

He continued down Clark street until he got to Belmont, turned and made his way up the steps to the train station. He still had a few dollars on his transit card, so he paid the fair, climbed the additional two flights of steps, and set up by the far side of the platform.

Darnel had no misgivings about collecting any tips. The station was abandoned, making it the perfect stage for an impromptu, solo performance. A few hours earlier, it was packed with rush hour commuters racing home to change, service workers heading out to their bars and restaurants, and college kids filling in the gaps on both sides.

All the city police and transit cops were preoccupied with the street-level debauchery, and the train-commuters were already where they wanted to be. For the next few hours until last call, the platform was a concert of his own design, intended solely for the love of the craft.

He pulled out his guitar and started strumming. The tapping of his foot against the wooden floorboards, the buzzing lights, and distant rumbling of the tracks, were a perfect accompaniment for his subversively intricate, and remarkably masterful arrangement of St. James Infirmary.

He'd just sang the line about putting a gold piece on his watch chain, when a woman appeared at the top of the stairs. She moved slowly and deliberately, as though she was contemplating the pros and cons of each step.

They stood there alone on the platform, two above the hundreds. He couldn't take his eyes off of her as he played. Her clothing didn't rustle or flap about wildly in the evening breeze. Instead, her pleasing textiles, and sensual accessories wafted about her softly, dancing and twirling, as the distant lakefront winds exhaled against her.

Darnel finished the song, and she clapped. She moved closer; her steps silent against the floor of the train platform. As she approached, her beauty intensified. She was a prepossessing sight of perfection personified.

"Tell me something." Her voice was hoarse and raspy.

"Yes?" Darnel responded wholly transfixed.

"You're young, but you play that old tune so earnestly."

"I don't think that was a question." he smiled.

"You're right," she smiled back, "Let me try again."

"Okay." Darnel chuckled.

"Shouldn't a man your age be down there in one of those the clubs, bumping and grinding along with the repetitive beat from some fancy drum machine?"

"Not really." Darnel scrunched his nose, "That stuff down there? It's not for me. I prefer the old tunes."

"Well, I've been around for quite some time. And let me just say, that was a fantastic rendition."

"Thank you."

"What are you doing on the train platform? Why isn't a talented fella like yourself onstage with a band?"

"I appreciate the compliment." Darnel blushed, "Actually, I was supposed to play with a group tonight."

"Oh really?"

"Yeah, up until about ten minutes ago."

"So, what happened, daddy-o?" she leaned against the railing, "You being hep to the jive didn't sit well with the band leader's modern pop sensibilities?"

"That's one way to put it." Darnel nodded.

"Well hep cat, can I tell you something." she smoothed an errant strand of hair.

"Of course."

"Just because something is new, doesn't mean it doesn't have value. But the classics are classics for a reason, and the most valuable things you have are your art, and your sense of self. Might not pay off now, or even later, but you'll be a lot happier in the long run."

"I hope you're right." Darnel agreed.

"I know I am." the woman smiled, "I used to be a singer myself. A long time ago. So trust me, I know how hard it is, to try and squeeze out a living making music."

"Oh yeah? You were a singer?"

"Hell yes I was. I could really blow, too. Should've seen me back in the day. Ivy Valentine and the Bronzeville Orchestra. We really packed them in."

"Ivy Valentine? Wait, *the* Ivy Valentine? The queen of the Black and Tans?!"

"You bet your handsome bottom. Oh boy, it was something back then. You know, I almost got to sing on stage at the Regal."

"Wow!" Darnel shook his head, and regained his composure, "What happened?"

"Same thing that always does, daddy-o."

"What's that?"

"My time was up. And when your time is up, that's it." Ivy looked off into the distance sadly.

"I'm sorry. I didn't mean to offend."

"No offense taken," she smiled again.

"Man, that must've really been something. Wish I could've been there."

"It wasn't all great. Us Black folks didn't have it all so easy back then. Even if we were headlining clubs."

"Yeah, I know." Darnell chuckled sheepishly, "But it's the vibe y 'know. People don't care about music now, not like they used to."

"Sure they do." Ivy smiled, "It's just a different kind of music than what you and me play. Trust me though honey, the way it is now, is way better than it was."

"Easy for you to say," Darnel teased, "With all due respect, you're Ivy Valentine. You've already been in the spotlight. You've played big stages. I can't even get a gig."

"Oh honey child, there's more to music than just bright lights and big stages. What you were just playing now was the best performance I've heard in a long time."

"I appreciate that." Darnel smiled.

"Well look," Ivy began, "I've gone and talked you ear off, reminiscing. You don't want to spend this beautiful Saturday night talking to about long-ago days. Now I want you to take this hear gratuity, or are you going to be rude, and make an old woman cry?" she held out her hand.

"Well in that case…" Darnel reached out and looked at Ivy's hand. There was just a single copper coin in the palm. He pulled his hand back.

"What's the problem," she scrunched her nose, "Why don't you take this here wheat penny?"

"Um, I mean, no disrespect Ivy, but if that's all you got, you probably need it more than me."

"Look here handsome, I ain't got what I used to have, but I can for sure spare a penny. Especially this penny."

"What's so great about this penny?" Darnel shrugged.

"It's a lucky penny. Wouldn't have made it as far as I did without it. But like I said, my time was up. Ain't no more luck left in it for me. But you go on and take it."

"All right, sure. Sorry. Thank you."

As the coin touched his palm, his head started feeling really heavy. He couldn't tell if the world was spinning, or if he was. His vision was blurred and there was an otherworldly, high-pitched ringing in his ears. He could just barely make out Ivy's face through the disorienting chaos crowding his head. She was beaming.

Darnel stumbled to the guard rail and peered over the side. The streetlights glowed with increasing intensity until his eyes hurt. He dropped to his knees, banging his guitar against the floor of the platform. Slumping forward, he rolled over onto his back, and lost consciousness.

Darnel was awakened by a sharp pain in his ribs. He squinted and tried to pull himself up, but then the pain shot through his ribs, and he fell over again. He grabbed his side, and lifted his head, just in time to see the toe of a shiny, patent leather shoe arch back, and crash into his ribs again.

"Hey Finny," a gruff voice rang out from above, "I think this spook's coming to."

Darnel rubbed his eyes and opened them wide. Two sweaty men in matching blue jackets, with shiny badges pinned to their chests stood over him. They held wooden clubs in their hands and snarls smeared across their faces. Their garments were distinctively familiar, but they seemed more like costumes than uniforms.

"What the hell?" I muttered.

"On your feet, ya bootlip." the one called Finny yelled, grabbing Darnel's collar and roughly hoisting him up to a standing position. "What're ya doing in this part of town, hm? Hitting the sauce a bit too much there, spook?"

"Sure he was, Finny." the other one smirked, "Y 'know these darkies is lazy enough when they ain't three sheets. Guessing he tied a couple on, an' fell asleep on the train."

"Hey officers," Darnel stammered, "I apologize for my state, but I promise you, I'm not drunk. I think maybe, just a little lost. I'm definitely confused. But I swear, this isn't a case of excessive alcohol overconsumption."

"Oh Eoin, you hear that!" Finny mocked, "Hear how he talks like a respectable white man? You're real learned for a darkie, aren't ya?"

"Whoa! Darkie?" Darnel thought. He considered saying something, but he was offended, not stupid. He wasn't about to get into it with a couple of cops holding clubs. Especially because he still didn't fully understand what was going on. "Officers, I don't want any trouble."

"Is that right?" Eoin sneered tapping the guitar case with his foot., "Well, if ya didn't want any trouble, maybe ya shouldn't have come over to the north side then, eh? Especially on the Lord's day, scaring all the good church folks with your jungle music."

"Officers," Darnel pleaded, reaching down slowly to grab his guitar, "My mistake. No harm no foul, right?"

"Ain't no fowl around here." Finny scrunched his nose, "What's a matter darkie, you eat so much fried chicken, now ya can't think of nothing but birds?"

"Yeah, we got a remedy to clear ya head right up, huh." Eoin snarled, raising his baton menacingly.

Darnel frantically looked around the platform. There were no witnesses. There was nobody waiting for the train. There were no ticket takers pacing about. Hell, there weren't even any homeless people that could serve as a possible deterrent. It was just the three of them.

Darnel grabbed the handle of his guitar case, took a deep breath, and kicked out hard. The bottom of his foot slammed into Eoin's leg, just below the knee. It wasn't hard enough to break it, but it through him off balance, and he tumbled into Finny, knocking them both back a few steps, missing the edge of the platform by mere inches.

Darnel barreled down the platform. He could hear the storm of expletives and epithets flying as they gave chase. Luckily, they weren't in great shape, and Darnel was fueled with adrenaline. He leapt over the turnstile and practically glided over the steps to the sidewalk below. He didn't have to look over his shoulder to know that the two cops were still after him. Their hard-soled shoes echoed off the iron stairs, providing an ominously percussive score to the chase.

He tore East down Belmont Avenue towards Lake Michigan. His shoulder collided with something firm but soft, that sent him sprawling. He looked up, not even registering that he'd crashed into someone.

All he could focus on were the uniformed silhouettes of the policemen approaching. Their faces were flush and sweaty, and their breathing was labored, but their eyes were glowing with the all too familiar fire of hatred.

"Hey there!" a voice rang out, "Officer Bohannon, Officer Garity, he's with me."

Eoin and Finny took a step back and looked over at the short, zaftig woman he'd bumped into. Her curves were unmistakably feminine, but she was solidly built, with dark hair, gabardine slacks, and a fitted, checked sport coat.

"Oh, you're with Ms. Hoover?" Finny smoothed Darnel's collar and backed away, "Well now, you should've said so in the first place. You almost found some troubles there, boy."

"Sorry, Ms. Hoover." Eoin walked over and shook her hand, "Finny and me, we was saw a colored fella sleeping on the platform. So, y 'know how it is."

"Not at all." Ms. Hoover walked over to Darnel, shooting an unmistakable glance that told him to shut up and play along, "It's my fault for letting him get up to the train. I should've put him in a cab. Tell you what, let me buy you breakfast. I'm sure Ronnie's got a fresh pot of coffee ready to go over on Sheffield."

Ms. Hoover reached into the neckline of her blouse and pulled out a wad of folded bills, barely held in place by a shiny, brass money clip. She licked her thumb, slipped a few dollars off the roll, and handed the cash over to Eoin.

Even from Darnel's awkward vantage point, he could see that unless Ms. Hoover was buying coffee and pastries for the entire precinct, she was covering a lot more than just breakfast for two racist cops.

"Thank you kindly, Ms. Hoover." Eoin smiled, passing the bribe to Finny who tucked them into his back pocket, "I was just telling Finny, before we saw your fella here, that we should get a bite."

"Well sure," Ms. Hoover smiled, "You deserve it. Chit chat doesn't fill the belly, am I right?"

"Right ya are, Ms. Hoover." Finny smiled, "Take care of your boy. Get him back over to the southside, before the parishioners finish mass."

"Indeed." Eoin warned, "We'll have a leisurely breakfast, but if when we come back, if he's still here…"

"No worries, Officers. It'll be like we were never here."

Ms. Hoover leaned against the brick façade of a nearby building and lit a cigarette as she and Darnel watched Eoin and Finny tuck their batons into their belts, and head off.

"Uh," Darnel stuttered confused, "who are you?"

"What the hell, boy?" Ms. Hoover spat out her cigarette.

"What?"

"You trying to get yourself a couple of shiners? Looking to lose a few teeth? Or worse?"

"No, I'm just lost."

"Damn right you're lost!" Ms. Hoover spat again, "I didn't think anybody would be fool-headed enough to be on the North side playing for change. Let alone fighting with a couple of coppers. Not with your complexion."

99

"My complexion? But this is Chicago! It's Belmont!"

"Exactly!" Ms. Hoover snickered, "It was only a few months ago, that those West Side riots went down. Hundreds of cops, over a thousand National Guard, almost 300 Negroes locked up, two folks killed- one of which was a pregnant girl- and that was over a brother trying to pop a hydrant for the kid to play in."

"Wait, West Side riots…"

"You think the pigs are going to take it easy on a cat spanging on their trains? And unless you can convince the pigs that you picked up one hell of a sun kiss, you'd best be getting back south."

"Hold up, what year is it?""

"What year is it?" Ms. Hoover laughed, "Man, you really did tie a few on last night. It's 1966, just like it's been for the past eight months. And in four months guess what? It's going to be 1967."

"No, no, no. It can't be. Look." I quickly corrected, pulling out my wallet, and digging around. I handed Ms. Hoover my ID, "See that?"

"Well, ain't that a Fancy card you got here…Darnel Lexington." Ms. Hoover looked over my license. Suddenly, her eyes widened.

"See that?" Darnel panicked, "You said it's 1966, right? I won't be born for another fourteen years!"

"Okay fool." Ms. Hoover shook her head, and returned Darnel's ID. She took a few long pulls of her cigarette, finished it, and immediately pulled out another.

"You seem pretty okay with this." Darnel remarked.

"With what? A typo?" Ms. Hoover laughed, "I done seen typos before. Never seen a fancy license like yours, sure. But I've seen a typo."

"It's not a typo!" Darnel exclaimed.

"So you're saying you're from the future?"

"If you're saying it's 1966, then…uh, yeah."

"Well time travel man, you need to get out of here."

"And go where?!"

"Go where?? Go back to your own time!"

"I can't!"

"Well, how'd you get here?"

"I don't really know. I mean, I was playing on the train. A lady came up- Ivy Valentine, and she listened to me for a while, gave me a penny, but when I took it, I passed out and woke up here."

"Ivy Valentine?"

"You know her?!"

"Huh," Ms. Hoover chuckled, "So you're hip enough to know the Queen of the Black and Tans, but not smart enough to stay sober on the North side on Sunday?"

"I am sober. I just…I need to find her. Please."

There was something in Darnel's voice that struck a chord deep within Ms. Hoover.

"Well, you're on the wrong side of town for that. Look time travel man, today is your lucky day. I mean, not for running into the coppers, and falling asleep time travelling and all, but I can get you to Brownsville. After that, you're on your own."

"Thank you!"

"Come on. Let's get to getting."

As they walked down the block, Darnel stared in amazement. The cars, the trucks, the stores, they weren't just different, but unsettlingly alien. This was an era forever unseen by those who weren't there to witness it.

Outside of empirical memory, any knowledge of the past is little more than carefully selected moments and images. The thick, rough textures of the clothing aren't adequately captured in photographs and historical footage. The font choices and artistic renderings of models hawking products applied to business names, billboards, and posters were vaguely familiar, yet the ubiquity of and repetitious uniformity of the placards and posted bills was overwhelming. Even the pungent conflicting scents of the congested streets was off. This wasn't what Chicago was like in the sixties.

This **was** Chicago in the sixties.

Ms. Hoover led Darnel down a wide alley, to a large, shiny car with sharp accents and sleek, low profile fins. It was periwinkle blue with a white top, tinted windows, and shiny silver trim. In the middle of its majestically curved hood, just above the broad grate was a chrome Ford emblem glistening in the sun.

"You like the car?" she smirked, "Guessing that even in the future they don't have wheels like these, huh? Hell of gorgeous ride, ain't she?"

"She sure is." Darnel whistled in agreement.

Darnel was still overwhelmed, but his uneasiness was tempered by his fascination. As they pulled onto Lake Shore Drive and headed south, his jaw dropped.

Where the towering, geometric behemoths of one of the most iconic and distinctive skylines in the country once stood, was instead a tepid landscape of as-yet unrealized potential. The Sears Tower (no true Chicagoan referred to it by the proper name) and Aon Center wouldn't be there for a few more years, the yonic stylings of the Smurfit-Stone building had yet to be erected.

They headed south past downtown and Grant Park. Fifteen minutes later, they pulled off the lakeside highway and rolled to a stoplight. Looking around, Darnel realized where they were. They'd just entered the incredible neighborhood known as Bronzeville.

Historically known as the city's "Black Metropolis", the beautiful lakeside neighborhood ironically began as the property of that notorious champion of slavery, Stephen A. Douglas. In the 1890s, the neighborhood began its transform into a thriving and renowned community.

By the 1960s, Bronzeville wasn't just a predominantly Black neighborhood. It was the epicenter of all things Black in Chicago. There were newspapers, restaurants, clubs, schools, and all kinds of businesses and artistic endeavors. They turned at the next light, and drove down the main artery, the lush and vibrant stirp, known as The Stroll. Darnel rolled down the window to gaze at the splendor of the center of Black art, life and culture in Chicago.

As they drove, Darnel couldn't help but stare at Ms. Hoover. He was surprised at how normal she looked. Aside from the texture of her makeup and that stiff hairstyle (not to the cigarettes she kept chain-smoking) she could've fit in on the streets in his own time. Darnel chuckled softly to himself, thinking how funny, and obvious, it was that people in the past still looked like people.

"Snap a picture, it'll last longer." Ms. Hoover smirked, "Something I can help you with, time travel man? "

"I'm sorry," Darnel exclaimed embarrassed, "but even in my time, I don't come across a lot of um…white women, who are hip to Chicago's southside scene."

"That makes sense." Ms. Hoover laughed, "I don't come across a lot of hip white chicks, either."

"But you're..."

"Not white. Passing."

"Passing?"

"Yeah time travel man, passing. Don't let my light hair and tawny tone fool you. I just play Ofay for my job." Guessing y'all don't have to do that in the future? That's nice to hear. Something to look forward to in my older years."

"Damn."

"What?"

"I mean, I've heard of passing," Darnel began earnestly, "but I thought that was more of a turn of the century practice. Like in the twenties and thirties."

"Twenties and thirties? Oh time travel man, it's been around longer than that. Way longer. Not really big news though. If you get chance to make more bread and open more doors by passing, it's not the kind of news you want getting around, or else that bread will dry up, and those doors will slam shut, you dig?"

A few moments later, they parked by a tall, seemingly empty building with political signs in the window. Ms. Hoover turned the engine off and nodded. Stepping out of the car, Darnel once again had a moment of music-history geek-slash-Chicago history fanboy shock.

"Oh my god!" Darnel exclaimed. Even with all that had transpired this morning, he still couldn't believe it. "Is this what I think it is? Is this the Sunset Café?!"

"It used to be." Ms. Hoover said sadly, "Ain't been a club in over 15 years. You know Cab Calloway got his start here? Bird Parker played here, so did Sarah Vaughn."

"Incredible." Darnel gasped.

"Yep," Ms. Hoover smirked proudly, "This old black & tan ain't jumping no more, but it's nice that all you future cats know your history."

"Not all of us." Darnel confessed, "In my time, most people don't know about any of this."

"That's a shame." Ms. Hoover lit another cigarette, "People should care about what came before."

"Yeah, they should." Darnel agreed.

"Oh well, that's how the river flows." Ms. Hoover sighed, "Come on now. If you want to talk to Ivy, now's the time. Got to catch her before rehearsal."

Darnel followed Ms. Hoover around to the back of the building. Even though he was still disoriented and trying to adjust to the reality of his impossible situation, he couldn't help but feel more than a little excited. 1966 wasn't exactly the heyday of jazz, but it was still a great year for the genre. Even the mainstream pop artists were backed by some of the greatest virtuosos of all time.

They entered an adjacent building through a side door, and walked down a narrow, dimly lit hallway to a somewhat large, but meticulously well-appointed and shockingly gorgeous ballroom. About a hundred round tables circled a massive dancefloor, the glossy woodgrain reflecting the pristine and shiny instruments resting on the bandstand. It was exquisite, dignified, and hard to believe that this whole space used to be an automotive garage.

"Have a seat." Ms. Hoover motioned towards one of the tables. She crossed the empty room to a door in the back and knocked. A well-dressed quartet of musicians came out laughing and smoking. They stared at Darnel, but otherwise didn't break stride heading towards the stage. A familiar sultry voice rang out from behind Darnel. He turned and found himself face to face with a younger version of the woman from the train platform. It was Ivy Valentine.

In the bright light of the morning sun pouring through the windows, her features were even more immaculate. Her skin was as smooth as an undisturbed lake. Every contour of curve of her face, chin, cheeks, and neck was flawless. Her clothing, that seemed antiquatedly bohemian in the mid-nineties, looked crisp, clean, and stylish now. Her comparatively youthful gaze was just as welcomingly unsettling as it was coming from the older version of herself.

"Ivy Valentine!" Darnel gasped.

"I'm sure you have a lot of questions." Ivy arched a perfectly maintained eyebrow, taking a seat next to him.

When Ivy spoke, the jovial demeanor of the musicians on stage immediately melted into the coolly detached, but oddly approachable, strand of professionalism that comes naturally to all jazz musicians and afficionados.

"I'm just...how is this possible?" Darnel asked.

, "You fellas, why don't you run through some warmups, while I talk to my guest." Ivy motioned to the band. They nodded and obeyed. She turned back to Darnel, "You want to know how it's possible?"

"Oh yeah!" Darnel replied eagerly, "Really I want to know if you can get me back. But I'm also curious as to how you got me here in the first place."

"You from Chicago?"

"Yes."

"So, you know Lower and Upper Wacker Drive?"

"Um, sort of."

"That's what this really is. All those science fiction stories in the pulp magazines make it sound like you can go back and forth like you're running around a hallway. Go forward? The future. Go back? That's the past. But that's not how it time works. It's more like layers on a cake. What we think of as 'time' is always happening, concurrently."

"Concurrently?"

"It means, at the same time." Ivy smirked.

"I know that." Darnel muttered.

"It's all a matter of perception. Once something happens, it ceases to exist in our range of perception. But it continues outside of our view, on an infinite loop in a different plane. You still with me?"

"Yeah, I think so."

"So, if you can traverse those planes, you can travel to any moment, because the moment has, will, and is already happening. Do you understand what I'm saying?"

"I'm pretty sure I do. But what does that have to do with why I traversed those planes?"

"I'm not sure yet."

"What do you mean, not sure? I'm here because Ivy Valentine- you- brought me here!"

"I'm not actually Ivy Valentine. I mean I am, but I'm not the woman you met on the Belmont Station train platform almost half a century from now."

"Okay I'm lost. That's not you in the future?"

"Yes it is, but also no." Ivy smiled sympathetically.

"Now I'm really lost."

"See, all those planes of time have different versions of me. There's me now. There's me as an old woman. There's me as a kid. Hell, there's me as I was yesterday."

"But you knew me. You know my name."

"That's because I'm able to communicate with a few different versions of me throughout time. I found out about you just a few moments before you and Ms. Hoover came walking into the club."

"I can't deny what I'm seeing, and where I am, but if you can move things through the different planes of time, why didn't you just come back with me?"

"Ah, see that's the catch. There's always a catch. Two versions of yourself can't exist in the same plane."

"Why not?"

"I don't know." Ivy shrugged.

"What do you mean, you don't know?!"

"It just doesn't work like that."

"How can you not know?!" Darnel cried, his voice jumping up a few octaves.

"You came here in Ms. Hoover's gorgeous ride, right? You know what's under the hood of that fine automobile?"

"I don't know" Darnel sniffed, "like, the engine and battery, and belts and stuff."

"Yes. The engine and stuff. But do you know how all of it works?"

"Not really."

"But you know how to drive a car, right? You can tell when something's wrong with it? You don't everything about it, but you know enough that you can use it."

"I get it." Darnel nodded, "I'm sorry. I'm still overwhelmed. I still don't know why you brought me here."

"Isn't it obvious?" Ivy shook her head, "Music. And you must be pretty damn good too, because I've got a great ear for talent."

"But lots of people can play." Darnel brushed off the flattery, "Why me?"

"You must have said something that made older me think you'd be interested in this opportunity."

"I mean sure," Darnel panicked, "I complained about the music and tastes in my time, but I was just venting, you know? Wishful thinking and all that."

"And the older version of me granted your wish?" Ivy arched an eyebrow with a slight smile.

"I guess. But I don't know what to do in the Sixties!" Darnel's voice broke, "I couldn't get a gig in my own time."

"Oh honey child," Ivy rubbed his shoulder compassionately, "I can get you a gig."

"Can't you just send me back?" Darnel wiped the tears from his face.

"You still got that penny?"

"Damn!" Darnel frantically began checking his pockets, "Must've fallen out back at the train station."

"Didn't older me tell you it was a special penny?" Ivy pulled her hand back.

"I didn't know it was a time machine!" Darnel yelled, "And I didn't know I'd be waking up on the train platform getting the snot kicked out of me by a couple of cops!"

"Alright, calm down." Ivy stated firmly, "If the penny is gone, you may be stuck here."

"Stuck here!" Darnel hung his head.

"Darnel," Ivy soothed him, "I told you, I can get you a gig. Listen to the boys in the band play. You can be part of that. You've got a chance to do what you love. Sure, it ain't ideal, but you get to do what you do."

"You have the most amazing ability in the history of mankind, and you just use it for musicians?" Darnel was near hysterical, "talk about a wasted opportunity!"

"How so?" Ivy responded angrily.

"You could use this technology to like, change the world- for the better!"

"Oh really?" Ivy retorted, her voice drenched in annoyance, "And just how in the hell could I do that?"

"What?"

"You heard me. Tell me how I could change the world?"

"Well for starters, uh…" Darnel stammered, "This is 1966, right? There's a ton going on, right? Social change and protests and demonstrations and all that. We've got the Civil Rights movement in full swing."

"Yes, we do."

"Well, you could warn people about assassinations or--"

"Let me stop you right there." Ivy put her hand up, "You don't think I thought of all that?"

"Well, uh…"

"I'm just a colored woman on the Southside of Chicago trying to make music. Future versions of me have told me all kinds of things. And yes, when we first discovered the power of the penny, we did try to do something. But do you know what they call a black woman trying to earnestly warn people about the future?"

"Uh, no?"

"Crazy. They call her crazy." now it was Ivy's turn to get upset, "You try to warn somebody about an assassination, and you become a suspect. There's a version of me that's spending months rotting away in an institution because she had a little too much info, told a few too many people, and drew too much attention to herself. So spare me your self-righteous delusions of changing the world."

"I'm sorry. I just thought…"

"Well you thought wrong. Bigots ain't going to stop being bigots because a hip negro tells them to. Cops ain't going to stop beating, harassing, and killing us, just because we say they shouldn't. The world ain't changing. But we can grab a little slice of the pie. And hopefully our little slice helps others get a little bigger slice, and so on."

"Damn.' Darnel slumped back in his seat.

"Yeah, damn." Ivy spat, "It ain't much, but it's way more than most, you dig? So, you want to play, or you want to try your luck on the streets of 1966, screaming about how you're from the future."

She was absolutely right. Not just right, but that last sentence held so much truth it was damned near gospel, and Darnel knew it. He stood and picked up his guitar case.

"Stage left or right, where do you want me to stand?"

ROD STRING NAIL CLOTH

CAPTAIN MICHAELA

ROD STRING NAIL CLOTH

T 'was a couple Venusian years ago
That this tale I will tell you took place.
When Captain Michaela, the best in the fleet
Simply vanished, not leaving a trace.

Her crew was on leave, when a message received
Warned of dire and imminent threat.
Captain Michaela tore off to the helm
And a most direct course she did set.

Michaela was usually not this impulsive
But this was a most unique case.
The identity code of the ominous note
Held a truly unsettling trait.

Though encoded correctly, the sender could not be
Authentic, it must've been blurred.
Decoding the code made Michaela's blood cold
For the signature on it was hers.

The time of transmission raised much more suspicion
Michaela sat pondering how
She couldn't believe that the signal received
Had been sent forty-two years from now?

The signal source showed it'd been sent from Arcturus
The fourth brightest star in Earth's sky.
They'd sent many a probe and all of them showed
That nothing was out there but the light.

The message said she was the spark of ignition,
The answer to trillions of questions.
But authorities tainted her noble endeavors,
So this was her final confession.

"My name is Catherine Okoye Michaela,
For years I have served the fleet well.
I've tried to empanel, through all the right channels
No options left but to inveigle.

My skills diacritic, acute, and prolific
Interdisciplinary glissade.
Your approach paralytic, your aims parasitic
With effects that won't quickly abrade

Two thousand, one hundred, eighty-four weeks ago
When my crew is down on the surface
I'll redirect flow, until the fleet blows
And I'll have fulfilled the fleet's purpose.

ROD STRING NAIL CLOTH

Calendars? Nothing but numbers and boxes
Though brandished about like a sword
Dates slashing away with a reckless impertinence
Forcing us all to move forward

For tomorrow comes not when the current day ends
The passage of time is illusion
That which once was, could also be now
Yet we need this collective delusion?

We created some metrics and markers aplenty
To reign in the infinite scope.
Of something that never was ours to begin with,
Nor something that we're fit to cope.

The question is whether you'll ever discover
The purpose of my machinations.
It's unlikely you will, since you'll likely be dead
By the time my work comes to fruition

In the kingdom of hours, I've witnessed the moments
We attempted our futile confinement
The continuum ignores us, but also implores us
To extinction, and further realignment

The concept of future is merely a promise
But not made to whom you may think.
Eternity's utterly far more important
We humans are just out of sync."

Some say Michaela had merely gone crazy
While others say she was coerced
Either way, we'll never know if Michaela
Had saved us from something much worse

ROD STRING NAIL CLOTH

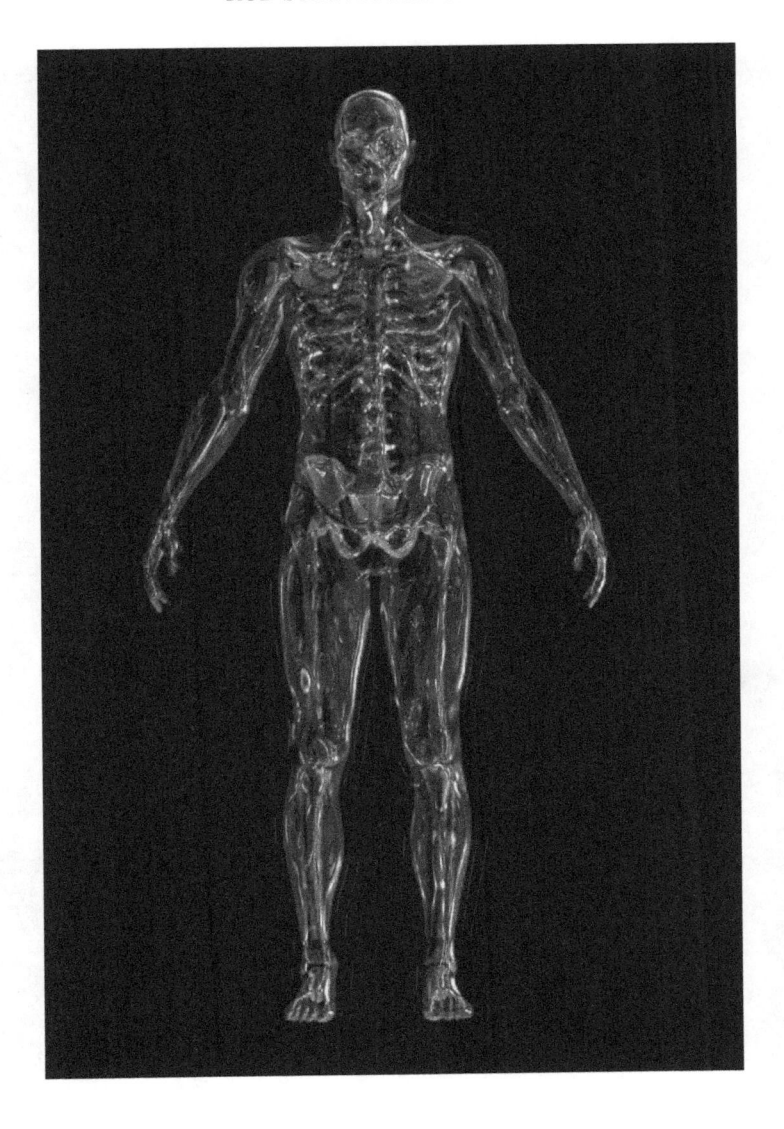

ROD STRING NAIL CLOTH

From: Ruby, Delvin
Sent: Wednesday, July 25, 2091
To: Singer, Autumn.
Subject: Hope this finds you

Dear Autumn,

I'm writing this now because quite honestly, I'm not sure when, or if, I'll be able to get communicate in any way, let alone write a message. I've been traveling so far for so long, the distinction between duration and dimension is practically nonexistent. My original trajectory has become an ouroboros. I've lost my point of origination and have no recollection of my target destination. Even now, while I hastily scrawling my thoughts on these sheets, I know that I'm still moving. I'm everywhere and nowhere, but hopefully these letters will find their way to you.

I don't know what they told your mother, or what she in turn told you, but please know that I alone am responsible. I knew the risks- hell, I developed the simulation models- but something compelled me to continue. I hope that by sharing my account, you will understand the truth.

Please bear with me, as I'm still trying to get the hang of this. To give you a sense of what I'm going through, yesterday it was 1989 and I was eight years old, getting eaten alive by mosquitos on a summer evening in the park, surrounded by tens of thousands of my fellow citizens impatiently waiting for the fireworks program to start. I locked eyes with a pair of bright blue eyes beneath sweaty red bangs. She was sitting two rows away, and the fireworks above were drowned out by her mellifluous gaze, but I wanted to say something to her. Then the sky folded and bursts, and I woke up at home the morning after my forty-fifth birthday trying to get ready for my assignment.

That's my life now. Even though I'm not sure that life is the appropriate term anymore. I have a sense of self-awareness and appear to have retained my senses. Even though what I see and hear, and feel doesn't seem like I'm seeing, hearing, or feeling it. It's weird. But I digress. I want to explain everything I remember before the lines of memory become blurred beyond recognition.

On that day, all those years ago, the assignment drone had ordered to report to ICT Platform Seventeen. I was confused because, as you might remember from your visits, there were only sixteen ICT Platforms. That should've been my first clue.

I confirmed receipt of the assignment. The assignment drone beeped in approval, and transmitted start time to my chronometer. Since I had a few extra minutes, I figured I could run over to the security gate, find a supervising executive and clear up the obvious mistake.

I zipped up my jumpsuit and exited the barracks. I jumped down the steps and jogged across the training fields, cutting through the officers' pavilion, and around the to the massive security gate, that allowed access to the road leading out to the ICT Hub Station at the far end of the station.

Just as I was about to enter the Hub Station, Morgan Whitewood came running up behind me, motioning for me to stop. Morgan was the Executive Coordinator of the Paragon. I'd never seen her in person before and was taken aback by both her imposing height and inviting aura.

She said good morning and we exchanged some formal pleasantries. I explained that I had some confusion around my assignment. Before I could go into detail, she held her hand up and cut me off. She already knew I'd been assigned to Platform Seventeen. That should've been my next clue.

She assured me that there was no mistake, and asked me to accompany her to The Centre, where she could explain what a Platform Seventeen assignment meant. Even though it was phrased as a question, it wasn't like I had much of a choice, so of course I agreed.

As we walked over to her transport, she opened the small bag and handed me a small, warm packet. I tore it open and was shocked to discover that it was a Yoma's egg wrap! I hadn't had one of those since I'd left planetside years before. It might not sound like much, but Yoma's still used naturally grown ingredients back then. I loved that even with all the breakthroughs, there weren't any synthies or supplements in their recipes.

Don't get me wrong, sustenance engineers are able to conjure dozens of wonders out of the food labs. Growing poultry in beakers, making vegetables out of regenerated particles, transforming all sorts of pastries into pills and capsules, but let me tell you, no matter how incredible their advancements are, no matter how nutritious the end result winds up being, they just can't stick their foot in it like Shayla and the cooking crew at Yoma's.

Anyway, I'm getting off topic. Morgan's transport was right in the middle of a no parking zone- but nobody would've dared to cite it. One look at the transport made it clear the owner had earned the right to be a scofflaw.

I can still see it clearly in my mind. Most transports are aesthetically pleasing, with their minimalist lines and sleek silhouettes, but this was a magnificent blend of engineering and design. It didn't sit by the curb, so much as it lounged on the street, basking in the glow of the filtered, artificial sunlight. Its' curved chassis was streamlined and svelte, resting upon the four, large, center-less wheels in the back, flowing down at a strikingly beautiful angle to the two smaller wheels in the front, giving it a sleek and speedy appearance even when motionless.

I didn't get many opportunities to drive often, but I thoroughly enjoyed myself when she did. I slid into the plush cushioning of the seat. Pressing the brass-lined ignition button, I let my fingers linger on the hand-carved Sapele wood appointments of the dash. Morgan explained that the entire central thoroughfare had been cleared, for our travel, so I could open up and really punch it.

I leaned forward and tapped the control buttons on the dash, setting the velocimeter to maximum. As we sped down the massive tube that connected the Orbiting Stations known as the thoroughfare, I forced myself to concentrate on the road ahead, trying to ignore the fact that the second most powerful person on the planet was just twenty two inches away, reclining back in the passenger seat.

I remember a few minutes into the drive, adjusting the rearview mirror, and catching a glimpse of my reflection. Even beneath the perpetual cloud of exhaustion, weighing down my features, I still tried to keep up a serious and professional appearance. But it was getting harder and harder every year.

Just after you were born, I was an enthusiastic new hire, recruited just a few years after grad school to begin training as a Paragon. It wasn't my first choice, but I'd figured I could use the experience and contacts to achieve my ultimate goal of acquiring a temporal relocation permit.

My dream then was to work in the ecological restoration, and I figured working for Elpis Network would be mutually beneficial. I mean, Lavell Douglas was a living legend, and the company was named after the Greek Goddess of hope. Talk about a positive sign! Besides, I'd figured this it'd be a temporary move, just a strategic investment. Spend a few years training with the top minds in the most innovative organization in the history of mankind, then leverage that experience into a top tier position doing what I really wanted to do, before returning planetside to be closer to you and your mom. But I'll tell you, nothing tempers and alters aspirations as dramatically as time in the field.

I'm starting to feel that tingling sensation beneath my skin. Which is the most surreal experience because I don't have skin anymore. Still, when I the barbed irons start tearing at my pores, I know that soon I'm going to be somewhere else. I'll finish this story as soon as I can.

Love,
　Del

From: Ruby, Delvin
Sent: Friday, July 27, 2091
To: Singer, Autumn.
Subject: More details

Hi Autumn,

Last night it was 1903, I was in a cold office in small country town listening to a sweaty woman in chains beg for her life. A few hours before daybreak, she claimed she'd heard shattering glass and anguished screams. She'd grabbed her father's riffle and ran next door to investigate.

She found her neighbor's husband swinging from a tree in the front yard, and her neighbor kneeling in front of the burning house with three of her four children. I was about to speak, but the air turned to syrup, and the sweaty woman's face shattered like antique glass.

I felt the tingles, then imploded and shrank until I was nothing more than a mucilaginous blob, melting in the dark. But I'm here now and want to make sure I get through the story before the tingles return, and I move again.

So, like I said earlier, I was driving with Morgan, listening to the calming whir of the wheels spinning against the hexagonal cells of the thoroughfare. The soothing vibration of the transport had caused Morgan to doze off. So, when we reached the perimeter gates surrounding The Centre, I had to leaned over and gently nudged her awake.

In case you've never been, The Centre is a majestic wonder of architectural ingenuity. To say that Lavell Douglas has an eye for design is a gross understatement. Before it was repurposed, it was the headquarters of Holmium Magnetics, the multinational company founded by Lavell Douglas way back before the majority of the folks in the Elpis Network had even been born. The gates were more for aesthetic than security and were a testament to Lavell's predilection for the number ten.

The gate was comprised of 10-foot-high columns that were each 10 inches in diameter and set 10 inches apart, curving outward at a 10-degree arc. Each column was wrapped in exquisitely carved marble, and on the sides of each were ten rows of ten nozzles the expelled and received the shimmering, pale green fluid flowing between them.

A 3.9-inch cube was embedded in the top of each column, generating a constant magnetoelectric charge to the fluid, rendering the gates both a wonder to behold, and entirely impossible to breach. The most welcoming place on the planet was also completely impenetrable.

The Centre was aptly named. As cliché as it sounded, this was the heart and soul of humanity. In the final days of what would later become known as The Last January, it was a terrestrial ark, providing the only refuge for a species three steps past the brink.

Back then (and maybe still now, but for sure back then), outside the confines of the Network, miles below on the surface, the air was toxic, and the water was lethal. The sand and soil were unsuitable for both hearty organic crops as well as the genetically modified, lab-augmented seeds that were supposed to be able to take root anywhere. There was still flora and fauna of sorts outside The Centre, but none of it was for splendor. Only those with the most hardened mutations had been able to adapt to unrelentingly hostile, extra-atmospheric environment.

As I was growing up, the ongoing conflict overseas had expanded into full out warfare. There was famine abroad, and hate-crimes at home. A rash of pandemics left millions infected. The unwillingness of the world's governments to enact effective measures to combat climate change led to accelerated evolution in a variety of mosquito species, which in turn yielded mutations in Dengue, Marburg, Zika, and Tularemia viruses, as well as in the nematodes that cause Filariasis, and the plasmodium parasites that cause Malaria.

No matter how you tried to spin it, the man-made apocalypse was absolute, irreversible, and worst of all, it was still in progress. The Network served as literal shelter from the ecological and viral storms.

While it'd be extremely challenging for you to try and find someone to deny the benefit of The Centre now, Lavell Douglas' tireless efforts to establish a refuge for humanity was an uphill battle from the moment he'd presented The Centre as the only viable solution. But he got it done, and everyone you know, or will ever meet has him to thank.

But back to my story. We pulled up to the main gateway and Morgan handed me her ID fob. I held the fob against the oval sensor and an opening emerged in the liquid wall, conforming perfectly to the shape of the transport. The second the back of the transport cleared the gate, the opening closed behind us.

Morgan pointed to a small area a few feet to the right, where a dozen personnel stood waiting, and told me to pull over there. That staff? That was the Archai, the personal security and groundskeepers of The Centre. They were just as impressive as the structure they'd been sworn to protect. They were all in peak physical condition, enhanced by various biotechnical augmentations.

From what I've seen, the Archai you might be familiar with now, haven't changed much. Back then, they were still dressed in matching agaba, a garment that centuries ago, was most commonly worn by Yoruba men. It consisted of an awosoke, a sort of billowy outer garment, an under shirt called an awotele, and loose-fitting trousers known as the sokoto. If not for their ID lanyards, and incapacitation pistols, the Archai could've passed for a crew of unnecessarily muscular yoga practitioners.

Six of the Archai surrounded the vehicle as Morgan and I exited the transport. Withdrawing security monitoring instruments, they proceeded to scan every inch of the car. The remaining six Archai scanned us. The beams of blue light emanating from their contact lenses was so bright, it made me squint. Once we were cleared, a statuesque woman with high cheekbones, thick silver hair, and caramel complexion, stepped forward with a polite smile.

She introduced herself as Zariah Melton, the Archon of the Archai. And told us that Mr. Douglas requested that they escort us through The Centre. Morgan asked if a full detail really necessary, and Zariah explained that it was a "mandatory courtesy," and then the Archai encircled us as we headed off into the main building.

I'd never been that deep into the Centre before, and had a hard time staying calm. Every ounce of me wanted to squeal, but I managed to restrict my excitement. After crossing through an enormous and gorgeously decorated atrium, we reached a pair of opaque doors that opened as we approached. Stepping through, we were immediately shrouded in darkness. If not for the blue lights emanating from the contact lenses of the Archai, it would've been impossible to find our way through.

The Archai lead us through the darkness to another set of opaque doors, that led to an empty room. The walls, floor, and ceiling were made of a material that looked like polished bronze, and the joints where they met were seamless, creating a disorienting effect. The only item in the room was a six-foot, black and gold tube that stood in the center like a monolith.

Zariah motioned for Morgan and I to wait here, and the Archai detail parted, allowing Zariah to pass, before following her out to through the doors.

I was as excited and intrigued. Whatever I was about to do, was definitely going to be unique, possibly groundbreaking, and my enthusiasm was tempered with a healthy dose of apprehension. But all those fears melted away when Lavell Douglas himself appeared in the doorway flanked by another group of Archai.

I know you've seen hundreds, if not thousands, of broadcasts and images of Lavell Douglas, but let me tell you, nothing compared to the real thing. He looked just as dapper and impressive in person. I still don't know how I kept my composure.

Dammit. I hate to cut this transmission short, but I feel the tingles flaring up again. They're pretty intense now, but hopefully that just means I'll be moving on quickly and will be able to return even faster. I hadn't intended for this to be a series, but it's hard to plan in a transitive, noncorporeal state. I'll write again as soon as possible.

Regards,
Delvin

From: Ruby, Delvin
Sent: Thursday, February 4, 2106
To: Singer, Autumn.
Subject: More details

My dearest Autumn,

My apologies for such a huge gap between messages. I thought I'd be able to make it back years ago, but this morning was amazing! I was just getting back to being me, all set up and ready to write you, when I looked down and found myself in 2792, passing by Upsilon Andromedae in orbit around the extrasolar planet, Majriti. I was hopelessly lost, as I'd never been that far out before- both in terms of distance and years.

To my horror, I realized that I was not alone. Something was standing atop a large, pulsating inorganic vessel. The figure was seven feet tall, semi-corporeal, and humanoid. It wore no clothing but possessed no discernible features to indicate nudity. The bright lights of the vessel softly reflected on the entity's lucent curvature. The being's skin was intoxicatingly lustrous, as though a sheet of blue chrome was wrapped around it. The head was almond shaped, and lightly porous, like a reptilian egg.

Three, blood red, streaks ran from the top of the head, down the left side of the creature's body. It was aware of my presence but sensed that I was neither food nor foe, so it didn't give me any more than a passing glance.

I found myself heading towards Samh and just as I reached the outer limits of the atmosphere, I blinked. That startled the hell out of me because until that point, I'd completely forgotten how to do that. But in the tenth of a second that it took my eyes to close, the tingles returned, and by the time my blink was completed, it was 1995, on a rainy day in the last smile of summer. I was facing someone who stood on tiptoe with her eyes closed, lifting her delicate chin up and to the left, drawing closer to the uneven patches of barely visible, fuzz on my chin which I'm passing off as a goatee. Her satiny black hair spilled casually down her neck, gracefully swaying across the contours of the valley between her shoulders. The chipped and chewed polish of her fingers crept out from cavernous sleeves, one hand deftly holding the first of many filter-less cigarettes that she enjoyed with an adorable smirk. Her other palm rested firmly against my cheek, gently guiding my chin.

With perspicacious concentration, I avoided allowing my mind to dwell on thoughts of that friction. That hip beneath the palm, the gentle hypnotic, swaying, the millimeters of denim over cotton, or the flash of flesh beneath the bottom of her shirt, the inches of skin peeking above the lip of her jeans. Concentrating hard, I was able to summon the tingles voluntarily.

It took some practice but in the span of an hour (well, an hour for me at least. Based on the calendar in front of me now, I can see that it's been nearly fourteen years for you), I was able to summon the tingles, and move myself. I still can't control the destination points or time frame scenarios I land in, but at least I can move at will!

I'm not sure if I'll ever have full control of the tingles, so I'm just going to cut to the important parts. In case you've forgotten- which considering it's been a decade and a half, is totally understandable- or have deleted/lost my previous messages, allow me to recap. I'd been given an assignment for a platform that didn't exist. Morgan Whitewood showed up and took me to The Centre, where we were escorted by the Archon of the Archai to a strange empty room deep within the heart of The Centre. Nothing was there except, Morgan, myself and a large, gold and black tube, and then Lavell Douglas showed up.

Lavell gave Morgan and I a quick refresher on the bounds of the theoretical proposition of the causal loop. In other words, in a retrocausality event caused during temporal displacement, a sequence of events causes another event, which in turn triggers the initial, preceding event.

Like killing an ancestor before you're born. Anyway, solving that issue was how he perfected temporal displacement, and it was the reason for the formation of the Paragon

I supposed before I go on, I should explain how the Paragon do our work. We use, -or used, because I'm not certain as to whether you still have Paragon anymore- but when I was a Paragon, we used Interstellar Interdimensional Consciousness Transfer, or ICT. With ICT, your cerebrum was digitized, and a model of your prosencephalon, or forebrain, is loaded into an extraversion launch machine, which is then sent from the Geosynchronous station to a reflector satellite, and then-depending on the destination- either transmitted into deep space for exploration, or converted to a tachyonic state, and transmitted to a receptor somewhere along the continuum.

No matter the assignment, we adhered to the three main points of the Paramount Injunction. Which were to uphold the integrity of the continuum, neutralize any and all threats to the integrity of the continuum, and maintain extreme discretion when interacting with any and all elements of the continuum, whether biological or inanimate.

All of that is pretty standard and could likely be found with a few minutes on a search engine, but what I'm about to tell you next, I'm sure nobody else knows. Don't worry, I'll put a nine-factor, bio-authentication lock on this transmission, so you won't have to worry about anyone snooping around in your inbox.

When Lavell perfected temporal displacement, and Morgan got the Paragon up and running, the original intent was to go back and change the calamitous trajectory of our species. But then, as you've probably already figured out, they were restricted by the boundaries of the theoretical proposition of the causal loop. The subsequent impact was impossible to determine, but the plague of apocalyptic conditions we suffered through the early decades were almost certainly due to our own meddling in the continuum.

Lavell and Morgan abandoned the original plan, and the Paragon shifted focus to maintenance. Things were bad, but the thinking was that maybe we could at least ensure they wouldn't get too much worse. That's where Platform Seventeen came in.

My assignment seemed pretty straightforward. The goal was to ignite the formation of a retrocausality event not within the continuum, but of the continuum itself. In order for our humanity to survive, we needed to compromise the continuum. We needed to compromise the continuum on an unprecedented scale. Instead of maintaining harmonious alignment and neutralizing potential threats, my objective was to become the biggest threat in the history of existence.

I was to complete my mission using the gold and black

capsule in the center of the room. This was Platform Seventeen. It was a prototype ICT machine. Instead of digitizing a cerebrum to send back a copy, Platform Seventeen doesn't digitize anything. It converts matter- in this case, an entire living person, and converts it into conscious energy. In other words, a digital copy of my forebrain wouldn't be going temporally displaced through the continuum, but rather I would actually be travelling back in time, all the way back to the very beginning of time itself.

But here's the thing, nobody knows what's there. Since the inception of the Paragon, we've travelled all over the continuum, but in order to maintain the integrity of the continuum, we've never gone back further than a half century. I was sent back fourteen billion years! I don't know if my mission was completed, or if I still exist. The line between consciousness, reality, and perception dissipated the moment I stepped into the Platform Seventeen and engaged the navigation system.

The tingles are coming on strong, and I can't hold them off. I don't know if any of these are reaching you, but if I'm able to send another, I will.

Remember me,

Del

From: Ruby, Delvin
Sent: Monday, September 6, 2117
To: Singer, Autumn.
Subject: please

It's 370 BC I'm here because I'm still haven't learned how to politely decline invitations from old men with authoritative titles. I sip cheap wine and stare at the collection of a young sculptor paintings. The work displayed indicates artists with passion, but patrons have more pretention than respect for talent. A hand taps my shoulder and I turn to see that...

It's 1996 and I see a face I recognize. I'd seen her around school on many occasions. She was a chain-smoking, profanity-spewing goddess among us mere mortals. The pleated black miniskirt she seemed to always be wearing, revealed that she was slightly knocked-kneed, although the fishnets over tights tucked into socks shoved into thick-soled, fashionable boots completely distracted from any superfluous notions of physical imperfection. Coupled with the same light brown, secondhand military coat, she was perfection personified, the archetypical example of uniform nonconformity that was all the rage back in those days. She opens her mouth and...

It's 14.1 billion BC, and I'm drifting at the crest of a wave of blackness so devoid of light, it's blinding. I am not alone but I can't see or hear or access any sensory information. I'm only aware of my being because I can still think, but my thoughts aren't my own. I'm not afraid, I don't feel any emotion at all actually. Whatever is with me is beyond the reaches of comprehension. I'm drawn to it because I am from it. It comforts me. It pushes me here to...

2117 and the tingles are pervasive and never ending. I know that this is the last transmission I'll be able to compose. This is the best I can do to give you sense of where to start.

$$t' = \frac{t - v\,x/c^2}{\sqrt{1 - v^2/c^2}},$$
$$x' = \frac{x - v\,t}{\sqrt{1 - v^2/c^2}},$$
$$y' = y,$$
$$z' = z,$$

Please find me.
Please find me.
Please find me.
Please.

    Del

From: **MAILER-DAEMON**
[Singer, Autumn]
Sent: Wednesday, July 25, 2091
To: Ruby, Delvin
Subject: RE: Hope this finds you

-----DELIVERY HAS FAILED-----

Your message was not delivered due to the following reason(s):

Transmission admin for the recipient organization has created a transmit rule restriction as the content and subject matter conveyed in the body or attachment material of your message is in violation of Interplanetary Interstellar Transtemporal Intercontiuum Communications Regulatory Edict 665532-2. If you feel this message to be in error please contact the Office of the Paragon Messaging Administration for removal of the rule restriction.

ROD STRING NAIL CLOTH

THEY BURN SO EASILY

Treat people how you want to be treated. That was the last thing my girlfriend said to me before she succumbed. Her words echoed in my mind as I gripped the handle of my machete, stuck my fingers between the dusty blinds, opened a small crack, and peered out across the pedestrian crossway, where a dwindling trio of Chalkies were rifling through the rubble, collecting the corpses of those who hadn't been fortunate enough to find shelter.

The low murmur of their voices was recognizable as conversation, but the words were indecipherable. Not that I would've had any use for what they were saying.

For the past six months since the catastrophe, the only sentiment they seemed capable of expressing was hatred and hunger.

The large one raised a child's headless torso above his head. The steaming viscera flopped out from the jagged flesh of the torn end. Steaming intestines fell around his neck, glistening in the dim light of the dawn. The slender, blood-soaked arms of the torso hung loosely at the shoulders, flailing about sickeningly as the other two Chalkies roared their excitement at the find.

It wasn't a pleasant sight, but compared to the rest of the desolate landscape, it was the only thing worth watching. The trio milled about for a few more minutes, collecting more disembodied remains, but found nothing as substantial as the torso. The amber glow of the sunrise peaked over the horizon. Shouting, they collected their trophies and sped off through to the ruins, keeping to the rapidly diminishing shadows.

I waited a few more minutes to make sure they were out of the range of both my eyesight and my rifle, then left the window and walked back behind the haphazard tarps draped over the exposed support beams that served as room dividers. The daylight wouldn't last long, and I needed to get across the river to get my captive to the secure area.

I ducked behind the final tarp, walked over to the bed and tapped her shoulder. She rolled over and stared at me. Like all Chalkies, she never blinked. Her cloudy, milky eyes stared at me solemnly.

Her emaciated form was sprawled across the plain mattress. No blankets. No sheets. Just a spattering of stains and pools were various fluids had hastily liberated themselves from her various orifices.

The men I'd come across last night lay dead around her. I hated Chalkies as much as anyone. But there was a limit to how much vengeful cruelty I would allow. Torture for information is necessary. Retaliatory mutilation is understandable. Under the circumstances, I could rationalize even the most barbaric actions. But when I came across the camp, and saw two of them pinning her down, and the third leering over her with his pants around his ankles, there was no question- and no justification- for what they were planning to do.

When they saw me, they spat out a thousand and one flimsy excuses. They hemmed and hawed and begged and pleaded. I didn't say anything. I didn't have to. I expressed my revulsion of their intent clearly, conveying my feelings on the matter with 15-inches of serrated, high carbon steel.

When I'd finished with them, I covered her exposed flesh, secured her bindings and dragged their bodies to the edge of the mattress. She was unconscious then, but if she woke up during the night and got hungry, she wouldn't make any noise, and- more importantly- she could feed on something besides me.

Chalkies were the infection's grand finale. While everyone who'd contracted the previous strains fell ill, it was only those with lower amounts of pigment and melanosomes that were granted superhuman strength and speed by the later mutations. In the final stages, they didn't live long, and needed to consume more human muscle tissue to survive. She hadn't fully succumbed to the infection, but the gaping holes in their carcasses, and the flecks of blood and tissue around her pallid lips, indicated that she'd helped herself to more than just a few bites.

The clothing hung about her emaciated frame in tatters. It barely covered her. I made a mental note to stop by the remains of the shops on Nicollet. They'd been ransacked pretty thoroughly, but hopefully we'd find something that would suffice.

I kneeled, and slowly gestured to the windows beyond the tarp. She cocked her head and looked where I'd pointed. Turning her face back to me, she slowly nodded. I didn't know if I could help her, but even in the tainted recesses of her mind, she knew her odds were better coming with me.

As we stepped out, she screamed. She was getting worse. Her exposed flesh blistered instantly in the chilly morning air. The infected were extremely sensitive to sunlight. Their condition granted them all the benefits of both vampires and zombies, but it had also cursed them with the weaknesses as well.

Taking off my jacket I threw it over her and drew my machete. It was too late in the morning to draw any Chalkies, but it wasn't them I was worried about. Another group of marauders could be near. They weren't all rapists and sociopaths like the trio I'd eradicated last night, but they weren't all understanding either. And the percentage of people I'd encountered that shared my preference of rehabilitation over eradication was extremely small.

After making sure we were clear, I touched the Chalky gently on her shoulder. She was shuddering and reeling from the pain but seemed otherwise okay. I tapped my wrist and pointed to the sky to indicate that we didn't have much time before the full light of the morning hit. She looked at me and nodded her understanding.

As we walked through the deserted streets, I found myself in awe of our surroundings. I'd always loved the quiet of the mornings. Without human interaction, the flora and fauna had reclaimed the city. So many people erroneously believed that if you want to relish the beautiful calm of nature in the middle of the country, you had to leave the city and head for the suburbs. I never felt that way. Even before the infection spread, I'd believed that while the open spaces and sweeping tree lines of the suburbs might not have the views of the early sky cluttered and obscured by towering skyscrapers, the urban serenity was no less exquisite.

I was so distracted by our environment; I didn't notice the Chalky had stopped walking. I ran back a few steps and tried to pull her along. She refused and pointed. There something in the distance ahead of us, or rather someone. I looked harder and realized it was the figure of a marauder. Not just any marauder, it was my old friend Caleb, the leader of the Twenty & Odd.

Contrary to their name, the Twenty & Odd were a group of about five or six dozen people who believed that it was their divine mission to eradicate the Chalkies. They took their name from the infamous letter written by John Rolfe describing "20 and odd negroes" that were brought to Point Comfort in Virginia, on a Dutch ship in 1619. Five hundred years later, Caleb, and his followers, believed themselves to be the karmic reckoning.

As the Chalky and I stood there, trying to think of a way out of this that didn't involve violence, dozens of Twenty and Odds emerged from behind the abandoned buildings brandishing weapons. We were surrounded.

Caleb marched up to me confidently. I pushed the Chalky behind me and drew my machete. The laughter from the Twenty & Odd filled the empty streets with an ominous chorus of bloodlust.

"I thought that might be you." He smiled.

"I'm surprised you can think." I retorted.

"Surprised I can think, huh?" he laughed, "It's refreshing that to see you still have a sense of humor."

"Caleb, I just want to take her to the river." I sneered.

"Of course," Caleb smirked, "But my scouts said there were about a hundred Chalkies milling about down there. You hear me? One hundred. What makes you think I'm going to let you change that to one hundred and one?"

"What makes you think I'm asking permission?" I raised my machete to his throat, "We're going to the river."

"My brother," Caleb shrugged and smugly raised his hands in foe deference, "Look around. You're surrounded."

"And you've got a blade to your throat."

"I've got two dozen Twenty and Odds that won't have any qualms going through you, to get to her. Considering we used to be friends, I don't want that to happen. Make the right choice…"

"Sounds like you're the one who has to make a choice. She and I? are going to the river. Whether I open your jugular fist is up to you."

"Don't be stupid." Caleb spat, "You ain't going to kill me, and even if you did, there's no way you're getting past my Twenty and Odd. The river is not happening."

As much as I wanted to slit him all the way open, he was right. If I killed him now, his Twenty and Odd would descend on us. I was handy enough with my blade that I could take some of them out, but not all of them. Especially if they were looking for vengeance. The only thing they hated more than Chalkies was a traitor. The only reason we weren't dead yet is because Caleb wanted me alive. For now. I decided to try a different approach.

"Caleb," I began, lowering my machete, "she hasn't fully succumbed. Let me take her to the river. You and I both know it's only a matter of time before she, and all of them down by the river, end up in the final stages. At that point, I'll gladly go with you and take them out. Please."

Caleb smirked again, but then dropped the cocksure attitude, put his hand around my neck, and leaned in close. He looked into my eyes, and he wasn't a post-apocalyptic warlord. He was Caleb, the chubby kid who I used to skip school and ride bikes with.

"Aaron," he began, "I'm going to let you go. But you can't come this way. My Twenty and Odd are clearing the neighborhood. You need to go back through downtown. If you hurry, you might make it before the sun's too bright."

"Thank you, Caleb."

"Before you go," he sighed, "Tell me something."

"Okay."

"What is it, huh? They ain't human. And even if they were, after all they've done? Even before the infection, they'd been oppressing and killing us for centuries. How can you show forgiveness after everything they've done?"

"It's not forgiveness, Caleb." I said, walking back to the Chalky, "I'm not giving them a pass on what they do, or what they've done. I'm giving them a chance."

ABOUT THE AUTHOR

AUTHOR, MUSICIAN, PRODUCER, AND COSPLAYER, T. AARON CISCO IS A MINNEAPOLITE BY WAY OF CHICAGO. HIS FAVORITE GAME IS CHESS, HIS FAVORITE COLOR IS GREY, AND HIS FAVORITE MOVIE SNACK IS DARK CHOCOLATE RAISINETS

CPSIA information can be obtained
at www.ICGtesting.com
Printed in the USA
LVHW091622121021
700249LV00005B/224